CAMPFIRES
OF
THE DEAD

CAMPFIRES OF THE DEAD

STORIES BY

Peter Christopher

ALFRED A. KNOPF   NEW YORK   1989

THIS IS A BORZOI BOOK
PUBLISHED BY ALFRED A. KNOPF, INC.

Certain entries herein were originally published in *The Quarterly* and *StoryQuarterly*.

Library of Congress Cataloging-in-Publication Data

Christopher, Peter [date]
Campfires of the dead.

I. TITLE.
PS3553.H755C36   1989   813'.54   88-8422
ISBN 0-394-57122-3

Manufactured in the United States of America

FIRST EDITION

FOR MY FATHER,
WHEN I THOUGHT OF THE CHILD ALONE
IN THE DARKENED HOUSE,
IN THE WHITE-FLOWERED GARDEN

WITH TALLEST, WIDEST, DEEPEST GRATITUDE
TO GORDON—
A MAN OF HIS WORD—
AND NINJ, AND FRANG

BLOOD
AND
SEED

Maggie, Mom tells me she sees you now and again at the market with your husband and your two boys. Mom tells me you stop and ask how she is, how we all are, while your husband pushes the cart and your two boys shout, "Mom! Hey, Mom!"

Maggie, what is asked in your heart's heart these years later is answered—Yes, Maggie, still.

This life those years ago, Maggie, is how I still see you. I can still see you waiting for me, football jacket tailed-out behind me running to you. The window light behind you is blocks and bars through the yellow kitchen curtains, on the kitchen floor, on the mouth of you telling me, "Mom comes home at two."

The home sick talk of television in the day is what still comes from the other room, Maggie, that talk, and the smell of toast, toast rims on the plate on the couch. You sit, handing the plate down to the carpet. You undo your robe, looking me your look.

Maggie, your mouth is still toast, tongue, girl. You are still the smell of girl sleep. You are soft robe bunched under me and, under the the robe, the heat and smooth of a girl unfolding.

A car that is maybe your mom's car, outside and under the talking low of the television, is heard driving up and by the house where you live. You pull me neck down from behind, lettered football jacket and all, to where we fit as if born for this.

3

Maggie, I can still see your dark hair golding, your hair on the corduroy ribbing-up of couch, on and over my hand. I can still see your bubs out flat, the dark of the bull's-eyes centered. Shadowed lines, thumb-traced by God, parcel out your small ribs. Your lean girl legs come up, apart. The hair down there is darker, pointed as goateed beard. My knob-on is out. My football jacket is rucked up, the snaps unsnapped and shirts yanked up for skin on skin, for the knobbed poke-bobbing of me inside you.

Maggie, there is no going back now. Breaking you open, the fear is you will not heal better than before. I can still see what looks like fear, your head back, your eyelids pinching, your lips rounding out O . . . after O . . . Maggie, the gathering of that vowel over and over is what brings me on, that and seeing you in the breaking and making of this, our lives.

The yellow light crosses the kitchen floor to poke the carpeted dark. The talk of daytime television talks on. I can still smell the smell of blood and seed. I can still see the red-knobbed slit with pearly gloss spun out of me come out of you. Gobbed, glossy strands hang shining from me to you, from yours to mine, from your two boys and their bluish bloodied heads pushing out of you to the red-glazed daughter of mine the doctor holds up by her feet, the same daughter soon to be home waiting while a boy runs to her as fast as he can run.

Maggie, when you again see Mom and she tells you, "Fine, we are all fine," know that what is asked in your heart's heart is answered—Yes, Maggie, still, Maggie, it is still gobbed and shining between us.

ROSIE AND DELLA, SANDY AND BESSIE, SISTER AND DINAH

The flies have found her. All winter, the only flies were those dead in the cold of the window sills. Now the cold has turned to warm, the days are longer, and flies tick the window glass. The windows are raised. The front door is held open by daughters bringing clean nightgowns and cake, by granddaughters afraid to come in and happy to go home. The flies land here, loop there, find her and the others rocking and dozing. A fly lights on the back of her hand and walks a blue vein. The flies circle the rocking Mrs. Podolski and Mrs. Hatch and Mrs. Keck. Flies light on her sleeping face. Susan keeps the flies from the lips. One lights on the nose. Susan waves that fly away, then soft whaps a fly on the sofa with a rolled-up newspaper. The old woman comes awake.

"Flies," Susan says to her. "Just some flies. Go back to sleep."

Summers, when her and her grandmother and Tops the dog fought the flies, is where she goes: those summers of Granddaddy coming in hatted and dusty for his noonday meal. Granddaddy makes sure the screen door is closed tight so no more flies get in. Somehow, more flies get in, get on: flies that are walking specks on the basin where Granddaddy washes his hands, on the crockery in the cupboard, on the white-painted walls and the lace-trimmed curtains, on the black of the Kalamazoo stove. Flies are over Granddaddy's noonday

7

meal of chipped beef and cream gravy. Flies are on the blue stitching of the linen covering the buttermilk biscuits. Flies are in the melting brick of Brownie Girl's butter. The flies are everywhere in the farmhouse so that Grandmother says, "Claire, I will give you a penny for every twenty flies that you catch me and bring me."

After the last of the red-chipped beef and the buttered buttermilk biscuits, after the rice pudding with raisins she at first thinks are flies, after hatted Granddaddy has smoked his pipe and gone back to mowing the fields, she and Tops stalk the kitchen. She sweeps down a fly with Grandmother's fly swatter. Tops eats the fly, still buzzing, and looks like he wants more.

"Grandmother," she says to Grandmother pumping water over the plates from the noonday meal. "Tops is eating my money."

After her and Tops finish patrolling the kitchen, they go into the parlor. Flies are on the sheeted sofa and chairs. Flies are on the piano keys. Flies are on the family photographs of the newborn, the baptized, the gone to school, the graduated, the married, the gone to war, the come back from war, the once living, the once dying, the all dead. The flies are stirred from the faces dead before she was born. The flies come back.

Her and Tops go back through the kitchen and out to the closed-in porch. Flies are on the screen door's screen. Flies are up on the glass of the tall porch windows, too high up for her to reach. Flies are down in the porch window corners, flies already dead, the left-over meals of spiders. One by one she picks the flies up by crooked wings and legs. One by one she drops the flies in the dab of soap on Grandmother's cracked bone saucer. She shows Grandmother the twenty-two flies that Grandmother counts out. She reminds Grandmother about the flies Tops has snapped up.

Grandmother says, "Claire Fagan, you will soon be as wealthy a girl as you are already rich."

Some summer mornings of fighting the flies Grandmother says the kitchen is too hot. The heat of the kitchen will have Granddaddy sweating more than his work in the fields, Grandmother says. The heat of the Kalamazoo stove will have Granddaddy sweating more than the horses Pat and Young Ned, Grandmother says, and so, Granddaddy's noonday meal is taken outside.

Under the cool of the two pine trees, Grandmother floats a quilt down. Grandmother lifts the quilt back up before the quilt can touch the dead pine needles, then lets the quilt again float down.

The plates and pitcher of milk are handed over from out of the apple-picking basket. The knives and linen napkins are laid down. When Grandmother sees the hatted coming of Granddaddy she uncovers the sliced chicken, the peas, the boiled potatoes, the rhubarb pie sprinkled with powdered sugar. Grandmother napkin wipes away the droplets on the pitcher of Brownie Girl's milk while Tops, on the quilt at Grandmother's feet, snaps at the flies and the yellow jackets.

Grandmother and Granddaddy and her take their time with the noonday meal. When they are done, Grandmother clears away the plates and lifts aside the pitcher so they can all lie out on the quilt. They lie on their sides, on their backs, in the creaking and sighing of the two old pine trees above. They lie in the pine needle smell. They lie with Grandmother and Granddaddy holding hands. They lie with Granddaddy talking farm talk up through the straw of his hat. They lie with her petting Tops. They lie dozing until Tops rolls up and snaps at the buzzing of a big horsefly. Tops misses, tries again, misses again.

Later, after Granddaddy has gone back to the fields with Pat and Young Ned, after Grandmother has flapped the dead pine needles from the quilt, after Grandmother and her have gone inside and Grandmother has washed the plates and started supper, after supper is done, after all that and before her bedtime, her and Granddaddy do the last of the day's chores. Her and Granddaddy go out to the barn and to Granddaddy's calling Brownie Girl. The flycatchers swoop out from the loft of the barn, circle in the getting dark sky, swoop down and around her and Granddaddy. Granddaddy claps and calls for his good Brownie Girl. Granddaddy calls with his voice carrying over the pasture where Pat and Young Ned fly shiver in their skin. Granddaddy's voice carries over the granite stone wall going up the hill, up across the cleared land to the high pasture and to the bell clanking of Brownie Girl coming. She runs to her chore of getting Granddaddy's milking chair. Granddaddy sets down his milking chair near the tie-up rail worn smooth by the neck rubbing of long dead cows named Rosie and Della, Sandy and Bessie, Sister and Dinah. Dinah's Brownie Girl looks in, her Brownie Girl head big in the closeness of the barn.

Granddaddy says, ''Come on, Brownie Girl. It's me and Claire.'' Brownie Girl slow clanks her way into the barn and over to the tie-up. Granddaddy, tipping his straw hat up with the resting of his head on Brownie Girl's side, begins milking. While Granddaddy does the milking, she goes over near Granddaddy's workbench and looks at the long-handled screwdrivers lined up from smaller to larger. She looks at the sharp teeth of the saws in the last of the day's light coming in through the window over Granddaddy's workbench. She looks at the curling yellow chaff of flypaper slow twisting in the last of the day's light. The flypaper is thick with flies, thick with the dead. She looks at the sticky curl of flypaper and listens to Granddaddy strip the warm spurts of milk from Brownie Girl. Brownie Girl's tail swishes up the flies to buzzing around Brownie Girl and her and Granddaddy. The flycatchers swoop into the dark of the barn from the almost all dark outside and hollow flap around Brownie Girl and her and Granddaddy. A flycatcher, seeing what is left of the day's light in the window over Granddaddy's workbench, thumps against the glass.

"Granddaddy," she says.

Granddaddy keeps the one-two count of Brownie Girl's milk filling the bucket.

"Granddaddy," she says louder, "there is a hurt bird over here."

The strip strup of the milking stops.

The flycatcher, beak open, lies still in the wood shavings on Granddaddy's workbench. She hears Brownie Girl's bell clank. She hears Brownie Girl's milk foaming in the bucket. She hears Granddaddy set the bucket aside. She hears Granddaddy scrape back his chair. She sees Granddaddy loom over from out of the dark. Granddaddy takes the flycatcher into his hands and smooths the dark feathers down.

Granddaddy says, "Poor thing, it broke its neck."

Granddaddy says, "Don't cry, Claire, it did not suffer long."

There is also the summer of fighting the flies when Granddaddy takes to his bed with the sickness in his throat, stays in his bed, suffers long.

In the upstairs of during the day, she hears Granddaddy trying to cough out the sickness in his throat. She hears Granddaddy cough as she looks for flies in the upstairs hall. She swishes the fly swatter down the hall until coming to the open door of Granddaddy's room. The shades are drawn and the room is dark. Tops, on the bed at Granddaddy's feet, thumps his tail.

"Shhh, Tops," she says.

Tops quits thumping.

Granddaddy lies there gasping. Granddaddy lies in the sheet that Grandmother has floated down cool and clean.

The wind creaks and sighs the two old pines outside of Granddaddy's window. The wind lifts the drawn shade, letting her look at Granddaddy not wearing his straw hat, the first time she can remember Granddaddy not wearing his straw hat. The wind keeps the shade lifted. She looks at the blue veins clumped on the back of Granddaddy's hands. She looks at the rings turned around on Granddaddy's fingers. She looks at Granddaddy's closed eyes and open lips. She looks at Granddaddy's lips working as if trying to tell her and Tops something. She looks at the thinness of Granddaddy's face. A fly lights on Granddaddy's face. The fly walks across Granddaddy's cheek. The fly walks over to Granddaddy's lips, trying to tell her something. The fly is on Granddaddy's lips when the shade flaps down and Granddaddy's room goes dark.

She hears the drawn shade tapping against the wood of the window sill. She hears Granddaddy gasping. She hears Granddaddy telling her. She hears Granddaddy telling her how she will join him beyond the waters of the Deerfield River flowing down below the farm. She hears Granddaddy telling her how she will join him, and how they will walk together up the hill, up through the summer green pasture where Brownie Girl and Pat and Young Ned graze. She hears Granddaddy telling her how they will walk together once more as if after chores, and how they will walk together to where Grandmother and all her others wait for her, to where she hears the welcoming drone of her dead.

THE CAREERIST

Ever think what do chicken-sexers think all day?

Well, this chicken-sexer thinks mostly him and me and Sweet Miss Stringbean. Make him Billy Boillit, sometime mill rat, most time drunk, my best friend. Make me Sarno, chicken-sexer. Make Sweet Miss Stringbean Billy's sweetheart.

I think mostly of Billy and me and Sweet Miss Stringbean and working as a chicken-sexer all . . . make that as a chicken-sexer all night. I work the night shift. Working the night shift, once you know what you are doing, once you tune out the peeping, allows plenty of time for thinking. Mostly me thinking how Billy, my forever best friend, does what he wants whether he wants to or not.

I am almost happy when bow-hunting, although I never get anything bow-hunting, or watching TV over at Sweet Miss Stringbean's, although I never get anything over at Sweet Miss Stringbean's, either.

Sweet Miss Stringbean is almost happy when her kids, who likely will make her a grandmother before she is thirty, are also almost happy.

In other words, like everybody else we know, none of us are happy. If we are, none of us know we are. And *that,* chicken-sexer or not, is plenty to think about.

· · ·

But there is always the Legion and who goes to the Legion.

This chicken-sexer goes to the Legion before going home to . . . make that to supper and sleep.

The Legion's the same as most legions—the same dark, the same smells, the same smoke, the same TV shows on the same TV always on the same kind of shelf sticking out over the same kind of stick.

What makes the Legion different is Desperado and Billy.

Desperado, who works behind the stick, is what everybody at the Legion calls him. The unclean rag he wears to cover his mouth and everything right up to his eyes is why.

Billy, who everybody calls Billy, slumps on the stick doing shots and beers and watching Desperado's unclean rag suck in, blow out, suck in, blow out.

Billy watches and weeps.

"Billy," says I, "what's up with you?"

"Me and Sweet Miss Stringbean," Billy says. "I say marry me to Sweet Miss Stringbean and she says to me she will when I quit drinking and getting marihoochied up and getting otherwise crazier than I get."

"Oh no," says I.

"Oh yes," Billy says. "I say marry me to Sweet Miss Stringbean, or else."

"Aw, Billy," says I, not knowing what else to say to Billy.

"I say marry me," Billy says, "or else I'll get drunk and marihoochied up and otherwise crazier than I've ever gotten before, whether I want to or not."

"Aw, Billy," says I, because what else can anyone say to Billy?

You know where and when I do most of my thinking? When I am wearing egg-white booties, egg-white jumpsuit, egg-white shower cap in a just-hosed-down room full of peeping.

Other than the peeping, which you tune out after a while, there is no noise except the noise of what you could hear if you could hear us chicken-sexers thinking and looking for the tiny bump that means a boy chicken. Looking for the tiny bump is, I like to say, eggciting work.

This is the kind of yoke—make that joke—that us chicken-sexers say when us chicken-sexers say anything. Most chicken-sexers do not say anything while sexing, at least not the good chicken-sexers. The good chicken-sexers, like Emile and unlike me, sex about nine hundred chicks an hour. Every joke amounts to almost twenty chicks and forty cents less.

This chicken-sexer would rather have forty cents less—make that a whole lot less—than think what this chicken-sexer is thinking.

Everybody at the Legion knows everybody else from going to the same grade school, to the same junior high school, to the same high school.

As long as everybody has known Desperado, we have never heard him say much. Now he says even less. Now Desperado works the stick without saying anything.

After work and before going you-know-where, I watch Desperado's unclean rag suck in, blow out, day in, day out. I watch Desperado's unclean rag suck in, blow out of the place where Desperado's nose used to be, until Billy, drunk and marihoochied up at the Legion's New Year's Eve party two New Year's Eves ago, bit Desperado's nose off.

This chicken-sexer usually goes over to Sweet Miss Stringbean's before going to work. Me and Sweet Miss Stringbean and Sweet Miss Stringbean's two kids sit on the couch watching family-type game shows.

The couch and TV are just about all the furniture Sweet Miss Stringbean owns. We sit on the couch with the two kids, with Danny and Dana crawling over each other and over us.

Dana, the kid who is the youngest kid, wriggles around and yells out the right answers before the people on the shows can yell them out and way before I could ever do it. It takes me too long to think. It is me mostly trying to think and wrestling around with the kids with Sweet Miss Stringbean yelling for us to stop.

In other words, going over to Sweet Miss Stringbean's before going to work is like bow-hunting, with me never getting anything and being almost happy anyway.

Desperado is what everybody at the Legion calls Desperado.

Billy is what everybody calls Billy.

Sweet Miss Stringbean is what Billy and me call Sweet Miss Stringbean.

Billy started calling Sweet Miss Stringbean Sweet Miss Stringbean first, saying she was so skinny and her legs were so long and she was so young and fresh as to remind him of a young, fresh stringbean.

Sweet Miss Stringbean's sweetest feature, Billy says, is how those long stringbean legs of hers lead all the way up to her snap.

The best thing about bow-hunting is time in the woods. Time in the woods, going around with a bow in my hand, makes me feel, well . . . make that almost happy.

I think getting something, getting anything, must be like getting to be something you are not.

Except when she yells, Sweet Miss Stringbean is sweet.

Sweet Miss Stringbean is sweet for a brick-eater.

Brick-eater is what Billy and me call women with no teeth. Sweet Miss Stringbean has teeth, just not her upper teeth, the big ones in front.

Billy, my forever best friend, punched out Sweet Miss Stringbean's teeth on Sweet Miss Stringbean's fifteenth birthday. What Billy's present to Sweet Miss Stringbean was was to wait until me and the kids were not looking when he punched her teeth out.

Except for what Billy says and for what everybody at the Legion wonders out loud, how would I know?

"What do you mean?" says I.

"What do you think I mean?" Billy says.

"Aw, Billy, I'm not sure," says I.

"Are you Sarno the chicken-sexer?" Billy says.

"Sure," says I.

"Then think, you chicken-sexer you," Billy says. "Think what the bump that means a boy chick feels like, but think of that bump as big as the end of your little finger, and right in all that snap."

"Aw, Billy," says I, thinking of all that peeping.

I am in my skivvies making ready for sleep when I hear knocking on the door.

"Sarno, it's me! Come quick!"

It is Sweet Miss Stringbean, sobbing and sucking in her top lip where her teeth are missing.

"It's Billy," Sweet Miss Stringbean sobs. "Billy's gotten drunk and marihoochied up and otherwise crazier than he's ever gotten."

"Oh no," says I.

"Oh yes," Sweet Miss Stringbean sobs. "And he's got Dana. Billy's got Dana and says he's not giving her back except in pieces until I say I do."

"Call the staties," says I, putting on what is handy.

What is handy are the day's—make that the night's— egg-white booties, egg-white jumpsuit, egg-white shower cap.

"Get your bow!" Sweet Miss Stringbean sobs. "There's no telling what Billy will do!" she sobs.

"Call the staties!" says I, getting my bow and a handful of broadheads and going out into the light.

22

. . .

"Hey, Emile," says I during last night's shift.

Emile looks up, but keeps on sexing.

"Emile," says I, "want to hear a poem?"

Emile keeps on sexing.

"Here goes," says I. "Had a little chicken, she wouldn't lay an egg, I poured hot water up and down her leg. Little chicken cried, little chicken begged, little chicken laid a hard-boiled egg."

That fucking Emile just keeps on sexing.

I live crawling distance from the Legion.

Outside the Legion, in the light, is Billy's old ride.

Inside the Legion is the same dark, the same smells, the same smoke, the same TV shows on the same TV, and behind the stick, suck-smelling it all and watching it all, is the same Desperado.

Slumped at the stick doing shots and beers, watching Desperado suck in, blow out, suck in, blow out, is Billy.

"Aw, Billy," says I. "What's up with you?"

"Me and Sweet Miss Stringbean and Sweet Miss Stringbean's Dana," Billy says.

"Where's Dana?" says I.

"Dana's at my place asleep," Billy says. "Dana was watching TV and wriggling around and yelling out the right answers before the people on the shows could do it and now she's asleep."

"Oh no," says I.

"Oh yes," Billy says. "And now she's asleep."

"Aw, Billy," says I. "In how many pieces?"

"In one piece," Billy says.

"Hey, Emile," says I during last night's shift.

That fucking Emile looks up, but keeps on sexing.

"Ever hear the one about the two chickens sitting together in the chicken coop?" says I.

That fucking Emile never stops sexing.

"Well, there's two chickens sitting together in the chicken coop," says I. "The first chicken says, 'Bawk, bawk, bawk,' and lays a fifty-cent egg."

That fucker.

"The second chicken says, 'Bawk, bawk, bawk, bawk,' and lays a fifty-five-cent egg," says I. "The first chicken says to the second chicken, 'So? For a nickel more, for a lousy five cents more, I should break my ass?' "

Hey, let us not even talk about that Emile, okay?

Not knowing what else to say to Billy, I do not say anything to Billy, just look at him and at Desperado and around the smoky darkness of the Legion.

But Billy, he looks at my egg-whites and bow.

"Sarno, you chicken-sexer you," Billy says. "Are you my best friend?"

"Sure," says I. "I'm your forever best friend, Billy."

"Then load your bow and do me," Billy says.

"Aw, Billy," says I. "You're my forever best friend."

"Then do him," Desperado says.

"What?" says I, not sure I am hearing Desperado say anything.

"Do him," Desperado says, his unclean rag sucking in, staying in, blowing out, blowing all the way out.

"Do me," Billy says. "Whether you want to or not."

"Aw, Billy," says I, loading my bow and weeping.

I tug back the bowstring and broadhead and take aim. I hold back while the shakes set in, hold back some more, then let the broadhead fly.

"Hey, Sarno," Emile says to me during last night's shift.

I look up from sexing. I look up, thinking I am hearing something other than peeping.

"Sarno," Emile says, "why does the chicken cross the road?"

"What?" says I, not sure I am hearing that fucker say anything.

"Why does the chicken cross the road?" Emile says.

"I'm not sure," says I.

"The chicken crosses the road because the chicken can," Emile says.

The broadhead thunks deep into the stick and wide of Billy.

"Aw, Sarno, you chicken-sexer you," Billy says. "No wonder you never get anything. Try again."

"Aw, Billy," says I, weeping and loading my bow again. I tug back the bowstring and broadhead and take aim. I hold back until the shakes and the ringing set in.

The ringing rings more while I hold the bowstring and the broadhead back until I am unable to hold anything back.

"Hold it until I get the phone," says I, tramping over in my egg-white booties, my egg-white jumpsuit, my egg-white shower cap to the pay phone.

"The Legion," says I, getting the pay phone.

"Sarno?" Sweet Miss Stringbean sobs.

"Sweet Miss Stringbean," weeps I.

"Where's Dana?" Sweet Miss Stringbean sobs.

"Dana's at Billy's asleep," says I.

"In how many pieces?" Sweet Miss Stringbean sobs.

"In one piece," says I.

Sweet Miss Stringbean sobs and I just listen to her sob. Oh God, she's such a Sweet Miss Stringbean, thinks I.

"Tell Billy I will say I do when Billy quits getting drunk and marihoochied up and getting otherwise crazier than he gets," Sweet Miss Stringbean sobs. "Tell Billy now, Sarno."

"Hold on," says I.

"Billy," says I, tramping back to the stick in my you-know-whats. "Sweet Miss Stringbean says she will say I do when you quit getting drunk and marihoochied up and getting otherwise crazier than you do."

"Aw, Sarno," Billy says.

"Aw, Billy," says I.

"Do him," Desperado says.

"Don't think," Billy says. "Do me."

I do Billy. Just as quick as that, I thwack a broadhead into Billy.

Billy, looking surprised, looks at the broadhead feathering his blue jeans.

"Billy!" says I, weeping and amazed.

Billy fingers the blood darkening his jeans, then holds the fingers up. Billy looks like he just made the discovery of his life. Billy gives me, then Desperado, that look—then looks once more at the broadhead—then passes right the fuck out.

Ever think what do cow-manicurists think all day?

Well, this cow-manicurist thinks mostly him and me and Sweet Miss Stringbean.

Make him Billy "The Gimp" Boillit, full-time mill rat, most time sober, my best friend. Make me Sarno, cow-manicurist. Make Sweet Miss Stringbean Sweet Mrs. Stringbean Boillit.

I think mostly of Billy and me and Sweet Mrs. Stringbean Boillit and working as a cow-manicurist all . . . make that all day. Working all day, manicuring cow hooves with wood chisels and mallet, allows me to go over to Billy's after work.

Billy's is the same as Sweet Miss Stringbean's was before she became Sweet Mrs. Stringbean Boillit, or I guess I should say almost the same except for the new big couch I bought us when they exchanged the I-dos. It is almost the same, with us sitting on the new big couch, watching the same TV with the same two kids, Danny and Dana, crawling over each other and over us.

In other words, it is almost the same except for the

couch and for Billy and Sweet Mrs. Stringbean Boil-lit and me almost happy. And me—once I tune out the mooing—as almost happy as I have ever been, and that is plenty to think about, whether you want to or not.

CAMPFIRES
OF
THE DEAD

In this long low slant of hill country twilight they have gathered, all at one time, now, her living blood out of the going-back and the going-back. Grandma Julia May goes back the longest, and looks and talks it with the flesh wrinkling off her bones, with the skin where she knuckles the same brown as the skin of the piglet the men have spit turned, Grandma Julia May says, way too long.

"Come here, Sarah, and see your grandma!" Grandma Julia May says.

Sarah goes over and into and is surrounded by the old woman's warmth and smell. Sarah holds her breath in the smell of housedress in the hamper and feels the flaking skin, the sway of the big hanging bosoms when Sarah pulls herself out from Grandma Julia May, sigh breathes out, and looks up at the spittle strings twisting in Grandma Julia May's mouth.

"You are almost as tall now, Sarah, as when your Grandma first rode under most of the bad men and too few of the good ones," Grandma Julia May says. "Of course, that was when both bad and good were not riding the real loves of their lives, their Steel Dust and Wink, their Lady Ghost and Raleigh."

Mama, taking in the big macaroni bowl, says, "All right, Ma, that's enough of that now. You, Sarah Caron, find yourself somewhere else."

In the hill hollow of backyard where the late summer

cool and dark first settles, Sarah finds Uncle Brayton off and away by himself. Between sips and carefully setting the bottle down, Uncle Brayton cranks the ride around Lawn Boy. Uncle Brayton holds back long enough to say, "Hey, Sarah Bear. How about . . . ?" with the rest lost in tug and roar. Uncle Brayton holds onto the Lawn Boy while bending for and feeling for and finding his bottle. He steps on and swings over and sits on the Lawn Boy while holding the bottle chin-high. The Lawn Boy sends beer shakes out of the bottle's top. Uncle Brayton puts a stop to the getting-away beer by sipping some more. He lets go of the handlebars long enough for a back wipe, then gases the Lawn Boy out into the growing dark.

Back over in the last of the after-supper shadows of the China willow on the shed, in the snap of the coiled blue bug-zapper hanging Daddy head-high, Sarah is knees-to-chin slung down in the strap-busted lawn chair with Grandma Rose saying, "Watch yourself, Sarah, or you will jackknife all the way through and hurt yourself good!" Grandma Rose and Aunt Phil and Uncle John make three away from Grandma Julia May, all sitting around the supper table set outside for today. Sarah watches Aunt Connie help clear away the bowls and the tins and the waxpaper-covered plates of what is left of the black-bonnet beans, of the salt-pork-fried-string beans, of the zucchini breads and pumpkin breads, of the last of the brought-up-through-the-field slices of tiger-cat-striped pig, of Aunt Connie's corn-flaked chicken and maple-sugared yams, of there-is-a-lot-of-Grandma-Rose's-chickadee polenta left, of the two ears of the husked and blackened Indian corn, of the sliced tomatoes and cukes taken from Mama's garden of the raised polebean flags—and Cousin Walter's run-down-your-chin-and-down-your-wrists watermelon, and, "Aunt Connie, is it time for Mama's pie yet?"

"Not yet, Sarah Bear!" Aunt Connie says in a voice busy with the wiping of the checkered oilcloth. "But it's time for you, if you would, to go get little Marlaina and Stevie and tell them to come now and get washed up for bed."

"Go now, Sarah, sweetheart," Grandma Rose says. "And watch you don't hurt yourself getting out of that darn chair."

Outside the supper table and the circle of trying-to-remember old ones is dark now. Sarah runs through the dew already down and past Uncle Brayton's shirt riding in the steady of the going around and around roar of the Lawn Boy. Sarah runs down the deer trail, down through the over and over of the crickets, past the floating-up little ghost faces of the burst-open milkweed, down to where the trail bends near the big woods and where there hangs the coming-on of night meadow haze. Sarah hurry-now-run-flies with the fear at her back until reaching the fallen-down stone wall and thrust up darker than the night line of trees. Sarah tastes the wood smoke and sees the half-dark, half-firelit shadow casting tallness of Daddy and Cousin Walter and Uncle Baptiste and Rico and Stevie army-blanketed up and little Marlaina sleep-slung in her daddy Charlie's arms. Sarah runs up to and against

Daddy, who, without looking away from talking Uncle Baptiste, strokes the hair away from Sarah Bear's face.

Sarah stands with one dirty bare foot on top of her other foot in the safe, tall warmth of Daddy, in the talking and laughing low of the men above.

"Sarah, it must almost be time for some of your Mama's deep peach pie," Cousin Walter says after a not long enough time of her standing close to Daddy, of her looking up at Daddy and at these men with her last name.

"Even if it isn't, it's anyway time to head up," Charlie says. "This little one has had it."

Rico pours what is left of his beer into what is left of the banked-down fire. Daddy moves his feet in a way that makes you think he does not want to be anywhere other than talking and laughing soft with Uncle Baptiste. Rico starts out followed by Charlie cradling and murmuring to his little Marlaina. Stevie, army blanket all wrapped up, gets to pony ride Cousin Walter. They pass from the smoky clearing into the darkness of the trees. Daddy takes Sarah's hand still talking with Uncle Baptiste. Uncle Baptiste goes up the narrow deer trail followed by Daddy followed by Sarah with the bigness of the darkness at her back.

Up ahead of Daddy is Uncle Baptiste, making the dark between him and Daddy wider. Up ahead more is the bobbing-blur-of-Stevie face riding the up and down dark gray that is Cousin Walter's white shirt.

Daddy and Sarah move on, more idly than before. The night haze is almost all around them now, hanging

low to the belly-high grass. Daddy stops and waits for
the others to get on way ahead, while Sarah comes
around and stands inside the safe tallness of him, with
her back to the tallness and the strength of him resting
his big Daddy hands on her shoulders. They stand quiet
while the field haze moves around them with the feel of
large animals slowly moving, the ghosts of the horses
Grandma Julia May named maybe, or cattle maybe,
or deer coming up from down below the big woods,
stopping and grazing, switching their ears and tails as
they come.

Daddy looks straight up, and so Sarah looks straight
up, out of the drifting-in haze at what Sarah once heard
Daddy say Indians say are the campfires of the dead.
They stay looking, heads back, his hands on her shoulders, until that swimming-in-the-stars feeling overcomes
her and only his hands keep her from swim-falling
away.

When she is again steady on the no longer springing
diving board of deer trail, Daddy lifts his hands from
her shoulders and they go on through the rhythm of
night-bug sounds, up the hoof- and foot-worn way to
the backyard slip of wet grass. They go on through the
just-cut grass and gasoline smell to where they can see
Uncle Brayton mowing away.

"Go run for your Uncle Brayton," Daddy says. "Go
on now."

Hair bouncing, Sarah runs in the slippery grass to
Uncle Brayton hunched over white in the roar of the
Lawn Boy, to careful now, to shouting, "Uncle Bray-
ton!" to Uncle Brayton hunched over and not hear-

35

ing, to running alongside and again shouting, "Uncle Brayton!" to Uncle Brayton looking up and seeing Sarah, to Uncle Brayton gentling the Lawn Boy down enough to hear Sarah shout, "Come on, Uncle Brayton!" to Uncle Brayton shaking his head yes back at Sarah and shouting back for Sarah to go on over, that he will soon be over.

Carrying the news Uncle Brayton is coming, Sarah runs until reaching the shed. Tapping the weathered-smooth planks, humming to herself, she stops before stepping out into the backyard light, into the voices and the laughter; stops humming and holds herself back in the slanting shed shadow where she watches without being watched.

In the backyard light falling from up on the pole through the darkness all around her, through the shadowed trailing down of the China willow tree, Sarah watches Grandma Julia May in her red-holey-grandma sweater telling something to Grandma Rose that Grandma Rose's face says Grandma Rose does not want to hear but is listening close to anyway, and Uncle John *puff-puff* starting one of his cigars, and Stevie no longer blanket wrapped up and eating some of Mama's deep peach pie, and Mama and Aunt Connie and Aunt Phil laughing over something while watching Stevie eat, and Aunt Ellyn with her head leaned down on Charlie's arm with both Aunt Ellyn and Charlie peaceful looking down at their sleeping little Marlaina, and Cousin Walter and Rico laughing out open-laughs, and Daddy listening to Uncle Baptiste, and they are all there, all of them but Uncle Brayton who says he is coming over soon, soon, soon.

As she watches them all coming, she says, "Almighty God, Father of all mercies, forever bless and keep my loved ones. Forever bless them in their loving gentleness and goodness. Bless us all, O Lord, with Thy love everlasting."

HUNGRY
IN AMERICA

You start out hungry for a little cuntlet other than the little cuntlet you have waiting for you at home, and the next thing you know you are with a lot of cuntlet not your wife, a lot of woman who is a vision such as she is, who heats you even when you are alone, who says she does hoodoo you do not believe in, do not want to believe in, are afraid of even if you do not believe in, only hoodoo or not, believe or not, afraid or not, the next thing you know you are far from where you started out, far from the wife no longer waiting for you at home with the no longer long hair: far from her and at the place in yourself where all you have left is the knowing that nobody, that no little cuntlet, no lot of cuntlet, no hoodoo: not that you believe in hoodoo, and even if you did, that nothing other than yourself is ever going to save you from yourself.

How I first met Sansaray—that is this whole lot of other woman's name, Sansaray—was while I was working the Pussy Galore and the DinoSores gig and standing down in front of the stage in front of the wall-high, wall-wide boom boxes: standing around in my grays, my Shadow Security gray pants, my Shadow Security gray shirt, with the Shadow Security patch on the sleeve, and looking at all the jail-quail-little-cuntlet with the rock-and-roll look, with the rock-and-roll-all-in-black-come-here-and-take-a-look look, with the little-black-under-things-worn-as-over-things, with the high black hump-pumps, with the gold and silver sparkling on their necks, on their wrists, on their fingers: looking at all the kid-little cuntlet wearing what they wear, while me and the other men and women of Shadow Security were wearing what we wear: wearing our Shadow Security grays and standing between the kids and Pussy Galore's roadies with the tobacco chaws wadding their cheeks, with the ponytails hanging down the back of their Pussy Galore and the DinoSores T-shirts, with the belly rolls jiggling over their cowboy belt buckles as they swung hammers down on the fingers of the shake-and-make-kid-little cuntlets making it to the stage despite the men and women of Shadow Security, making it to the stage and trying to get up and over to Pussy to come away with fingers pointing several ways at the same time. Many of the roadies, at least many of the roadies I could see from where I was standing, stopped swinging their hammers when seeing this one womanly lot of cuntlet, this one womanly lot of something that from where I was standing looked to me like she was a lot of anything she wanted to be and later turned out to be Sansaray: that whole-lot-of-make-you-want-to-gobble-her-up-kind of woman; that whole-lot-of-make-you-want-to-jack-rabbit-yourself-until-your-fillings-fall-out kind of woman; that whole-lot-of-want-to-make-you-whip-up-some-hasty-pudding-using-only-yourself kind of woman; that kind of woman in her black hump-pumps, in her black stockings with the rhinestones running up the seams, in her little black-and-white

undersomething spotted and striped as if once belonging
to some big make-believe animal, some big make-believe
cat maybe crawling around in some make-believe jungle somewhere, and now, and then, crawling all over
her, crawling up her, crawling up Sansaray's vajaguar
so you could see the groove of Sansaray's vajaguar; see
that while seeing her big, her gigundo slurpies leaping
all over, and her hair—man, what hair, hair black and
curly and out twice as far, blow-dried out at least twice
as wild as any hair at the gig—her hair was almost as
long as my wife's long hair was, but black and blow-
dried way out; and there was also the gold and silver
sparkling on her neck, on her wrists, on her fingers,
sparkling all over her, while she, while Sansaray, sort
of humped, sort of rode the blast of sound until Sansaray, this whole-lot-of-hoodoo-or-so-she-later-said kind
of woman, this table-grade kind of woman, this schtup-
perwear kind of woman with her vajaguar and her
slurpies giddyapping all over her, reached up under
her little black-and-white-spotted-and-striped undersomething worn as outersomething—but going down
so far, just crawling over and up her vajaguar so far—
reached up and yanked down her little V-sheath of
panty undersomething, which she then stepped out of,
which she then balled up in one bejeweled *uh, uh, uh*
hand and sort of sissy-tossed toward Pussy Galore and
the DinoSores for the lacy little V-sheath of a panty
undersomething to then float, to then barely carry, to
then unball and land *right . . . on . . . my . . . head,* with
me looking out one of the leg holes at her, at Sansaray
humping the sound with ten thousand million other

screaming and singing Pussy Galore fans, not to mention the men and women of Shadow Security in their Shadow Security grays.

Meanwhile, the little wife at home at the time with her then long hair was trying despite herself, trying despite myself, trying with among other things notes left on the kitchen table starting with "Dear Fuckface" and ending with "Love, your wife, who loves you despite myself, despite yourself, and who is at least trying, which is more than can be said for some of us"—and despite the despites, she did try—among other things, tried pulling me into the shower with the hot water sliding down us, with the shower drain clogged and the warm and the soapy and the scummy water rising up us, with my wife's long wet hair all over us, with my mouth on my wife's mouth, with my hands on my wife's soaped-up slurpies, with my wife's hands on my soaped-up Elijajuan. With all the soap, with all the trying, there was still no *"Oh, Jesus, oh"* from my wife, just more trying with the running-out hot water sliding down us, with the scummy water with the strings of dirt and with the clots of Elijajuan juice rising up us, with the look in my wife's wife eyes turning from *I'm trying, Chet,* to *What the fuck are we doing, Chet?* until that *we,* until that *us,* became that *I . . .* starting out, going out, ordering out for a side order of what I started telling you about.

I was looking at Sansaray, the most lot of cuntlet looked at outside of a bone book, the most lot of anything I

44

have looked at while looking out the leg hole of a little
undersomething, while then taking Sansaray's little
V-sheath of a panty undersomething off my head, while
then handing the little undersomething back to her, to
which she says, "Thank you," says, "Look at the big
spook over there, look, coming over here with three
beers in each hand"; says, "The big black giant of a
son-of-a-bitch, Dacey, that Dace, the motherfucker is
driving me to hoodoo!"—while slipping around behind
me, while holding on with both hands, while holding
onto her little V-sheath of black panty undersomething
while holding onto my arm, the arm with the Shadow
Security patch on the gray sleeve; the arm that in high
school almost had a muscle, just the one arm and just
the one muscle from scooping, from using just the one
arm to scoop ice cream after school; that soft but official
arm under Sansaray's bejeweled *uh, uh, uh* fingers, when
the big black fucking spook with muscles all over, with
big muscles in places I did not have places to have muscles in, when the big black fucking spook of a man came
over and says, "Occifer," this is the way he said officer,
says, "Occifer, whatever the probem," this is the way
he said problem, says, "Occifer, whatever the probem,
I so big, so black, so giant of a spook son-of-a-bitch,
that no probem, that no nothing, that no nobody wants
to waste whatever little they got fucking with me"; and
I say, "Yes, sir, only this woman, sir, this whole lot of
heat-and-eat woman here, sir, is now in the custody of
Shadow Security for, for, for indecisive exposure in a
public place with an occupancy of more than ten thousand million people, sir, Dacey sir, if I may call you
Dacey or Dace, sir, if I may call you sir, sir"—when

the spook says real soft, says, "Occifer, who's zooming who, okay?"—and this officer, me, I say nothing, not one word more, while putting on my best I'm-bending-over-and-cracking-a-smile smile, while giving him that smile with the lower lip up over the upper teeth, while backing up, while inching back, with Sansaray holding onto the back of my Shadow Security belt, with us— notice that *us*— with *us* inching back, tripping back over some of the screaming kids with their kid faces locked on Pussy Galore and the DinoSores, with *us* moving as quick-footed as *we* could move backward with Sansaray in her hump-pumps, with *me* looking at the giant spook, at the big black muscle of a man standing looking at *us* tripping back through the crowd with *me* yelling, *"Shadow Security backing through!"*—until getting *through* and *around* and *backstage* to the band's way out, which was guarded by at least ten, maybe more, Shadow Security men and women, who let *us* back *by* and *through* and *down* the hall—and *out* the back way to the parking lot and *over* to the Shadow Security jeep, when Sansaray, holding on to the back of my Shadow Security belt, says, "How about a lift home"; says, "You look married"; says, "The hoodoo works in strange ways"; says, "Uh-oh"; says, "Look"; says, "Here comes the fucking spook"; says, "Drive, Mr. Shadow Security, drive."

I drove—headlong.

Sansaray sometimes, one time, talked hoodoo in a way that was enough to make you wonder when she talked about causing snakes and spiders to spring up inside

the body of somebody, although Sansaray said she only
talked that kind of hoodoo and was not into that kind
of hoodoo and that she was mostly, really, only, into
uncrossing hoodoo, into doing hoodoo that was against
hoodoo, and not really into snakes or spiders or anything like that, although Sansaray did say she once did
use a catfish that she had her brother Levon catch and
hold while she clipped off the three sharp spikes on the
catfish's back, which she dried over a flame, which she
crushed into powder, which she mixed with white pepper and then, she said, and then she then wrote the
name of the somebody, the name of Sansaray's second-
semester math teacher. You see, Sansaray was in her
second semester at Apex Tech at the time I am telling
you about—or so she said, and that she also said that
she would never do any hoodoo like this now, or like
that now, although Sansaray said she did once do this
kind of hoodoo to get a good lock on a neighbor's insides, so the insides of this neighbor could not even
come across with a Hershey squirt or anything for the
rest of his fucking life. Then she wrote on a slip of paper
the name of the somebody, this Mr. Amato, her second-
semester math teacher at Apex Tech. She wrote his
name three times across itself, then folded up the powdered catfish spikes and white pepper inside the paper
and put the paper into the mouth of the catfish, then
had her brother Levon throw the catfish back into the
same part of the river Levon had first got the fucking
catfish out of, and within a week, or so Sansaray said
to me, this Mr. Amato was teaching second-semester
math fucking naked from the waist down: naked with
his little hairy woman-bait hanging down, fucking na-

ked like that, until Mr. Sullivan, Apex Tech chancellor, and Mr. Lemoyne, Apex Tech custodian, hustled Mr. Amato out; and that was the one time, that and her neighbor's locked insides, that Sansaray said she did that kind of hoodoo to anybody, and she was now into uncrossing hoodoo, using roots to uncross hoodoo, using, she said, red coon root, Solomon's red root, Come Back In One Piece root, Cast Off root, Hurry Up root, yaw root, Jinx Killer root, and some other roots I do not remember, because by then Sansaray was making me think only of my Elijajuan root, more than she had already been making me think of it.

Meanwhile, the little wife said what she said by leaving off the light, so coming home late, coming home early, there was no light for me to see to put the key in the lock as quietly as possible, to close the door as quietly as possible, to tiptoe down the hall as quietly as possible, to heel off my Shadow Security boots, to tiptoe in my socks into the kitchen for a slug of milk straight out of the carton and down my chin and down my Shadow Security gray shirt to drip all over the goddamn kitchen floor, to read in the light of the open fridge the note left on the kitchen table starting with "Dear Numbnuts" and ending with "You and your secret Shadow Security night assignments, come on, Chet, who is zooming who?" to put the milk carton away as quietly as possible, to tiptoe back down the hall as quietly as possible, to leave my Shadow Security grays on the living room rug as neat as possible, to lower my 157 pounds of no muscles whatsoever into bed so as not to disturb the person then sleeping the way she then slept, with her then still long hair spread out on the pillow, with her sleep-breathing the one sound other than the sound of the fucking fridge, with the set of her chin saying to me in the dark, *Yes, Chet, you have pissed what we had away, Chet!*

When you find a little cuntlet that turns out to be a lot of cuntlet, the next thing you know you want to do, you want to go a little somewhere, like to Pizza My Heart on a slow Tuesday night to order the Heart Stopper, which, by the way, is seven dollars and change a slice. You order a slice of the Heart Stopper for her and a tall water for you, and you watch as the olives, as the hot sausage, as the shrooms ooze off onto her sweater-covered slurpies at their slurpies-at-ease, which you offer to clean off without using your hands, and to which she says, Yeah? So . . . then . . . you . . . figure you will take her to Donut Master for donut holes, and watch as she scarfs down maybe half a dozen at three-and-change a dozen before heading back out to the Shadow Security jeep and to sitting and telling her how *you have never felt like this before* and how you are going crazy to take her to some really special place, like probably to a Brew & Trough, but, hey, you are a right-to-the-point kind of guy, with the point suddenly being that you have got to slap a little Elijajuan on her right this very instant; then you say, in all *seriousness* now, with all *kidding aside* now, that what you really want is for her to throw a crotch-lock on your face until either her legs go numb and turn blue or until you drop dead from suffocation, whatever comes first, and this is exactly what the game plan was on that slow Tuesday night, with me wearing my best Shadow Security grays and driving the Shadow Security jeep, when suddenly I am out front of where Sansaray lives with her father, her mother, her grandmother, her four sisters, her brother Levon; out front looking in the bay window dark but for the flicker of blue on the glass, and me honk-honking for Sansaray, for that whole-lot-of-hurt-me-good kind of woman, for that whole-lot-of-even-learn-ballroom-dancing-if-that-is-what-she-wanted kind of woman, for that whole-lot-of-spank-and-serve-fucking woman, and then that woman letting the screen door whack shut behind her while she clacks down the steps in her hump-pumps, then clicks down the walk with all the sparkle sparkling on her neck, on her wrists, on her *uh, uh, uh* fingers holding a little kimono something or other up close to her as she clicks. I reach over and snap open the door to give Sansaray a hand in, as it were, when she says, "You know, you still look married, but not as married as you looked before, Chet"; says, "We're staying right here, Chet"; says, "You can meet my father, my mother, my grandmother, my four sisters, my brother Levon, and some others I want you to meet, Chet."

We stay.

I figure I saved big bucks by not going to Pizza My Heart, by not going to Donut Master, by not going to Brew & Trough and by going inside instead, but that leaves out, of course, totaling up certain costs, which you will see are to come later.

All the while, of course, less and less of the little woman was at home, less and less of the little wife—less like no washing dishes, like no washing clothes, like no cooking food, like no talking words, like no leaving notes anymore, like no fucking for the idea of home and hearth.

But I still come home and give her the "Honey, I'm home," and get back just the sound of running water until, after an hour of getting that sound, I go in and see her sitting in the tub with a scissors in one hand and a clump of long hair in the other hand, sitting with the shower water shooting down at her, her face all twisted up in the weeping way she has, sitting with clumps of long hair floating all around her on the rising, scummy, too-cool-by-then water.

We were inside, in the living room dark except for the big TV flickering *Fantasy Island* all over the walls, all over the ceiling, all over the faces and the hands of Sansaray's father, Sansaray's mother, her grandmother, her four sisters, her brother Levon, all watching *Fantasy Island* with none of them even looking up to see me when Sansaray says, "This is Chet of Shadow Security," with none of them even looking away from *Fantasy Island* when we go into Sansaray's room with Sansaray clunking the door and snickering the dead bolt behind us, locking in what looks to me like a big wind had come through and blown all of Sansaray's shit all over the floor, all over the chair, all over the unmade bed, all over and hanging off the antenna of the little TV rolling *Fantasy Island* we are now watching while sitting on Sansaray's bed, that little TV that Sansaray is watching while I help her take off the kimono sort of outersomething worn as outersomething over her white-turned-blue-with-*Fantasy Island* shoulders, over her strapless, shoulderless, cut way-low-way-down-to-there little pushup of a little undersomething worn as undersomething, while I help her unzip the pushup little undersomething's zipper, letting loose her humongous slurpies, while I help her slide down her little V-sheath of panty undersomething hiding her groove, her slice of hairy vajaguar, while I help me unbutton, unzip, let drop my Shadow Security gray pants, while I help slide down my Shadow Security gray skivvies, when Sansaray, without for one instant looking away from *Fantasy Island* rolling blue over her white arms, over her white belly, over her red slice of vajaguar, says, "Wait, Chet"; says, *"Fantasy Island* ain't over, Chet"; says, "Dincha hear the door, Chet?" when I hear *thud, thud* on the door and I hear her brother Levon, shouting, "The big black giant of a spook is out here with a whole lot of others, and the spook and the others want to fucking talk to what's his name!" and Sansaray says, "Tell the big black giant of a spook and all the others that we are watching *Fantasy Island!*" and Levon shouts, "You tell them yourself!" and Sansaray, without taking her eyes off *Fantasy Island,* gets up off the unmade bed and goes over to the little TV and turns up the sound and comes back over to the bed, when there is a *thud, thud* on the door and a *deep, deep* voice on the other side of the door says, "Occifer, I want to talk to you," and

Sansaray, without looking away from *Fantasy Island,* says, "Talk to him, Chet"; and the *deep, deep* voice on the other side of the door says, "Occifer, there is no probem that we cannot take care of if we put our minds to it"; and Sansaray, without looking away from *Fantasy Island,* says, "Put your mind to it, Chet"; and the *deep, deep* voice on the other side of the door says, "Sansaray, unlock the door"; and Sansaray gets up off the bed without looking away from *Fantasy Island* and goes over to the door and grabs the dead bolt . . . when I shout, *"Wait!"*

About my wife, you should know so much less of the less of the little woman was no longer at home that there was just a note left on the kitchen table with nothing written on either side of the plain white notepaper other than "Dear Geekmonger."

As I was saying, Sansaray was waiting when I shouted, *"Wait!"* and holding on to the dead bolt and watching *Fantasy Island* when the *deep, deep* voice on the other side of the door says, "Occifer, it is nearly time"; and no sooner does the *deep, deep* voice on the other side of the door say that than the theme music for *Fantasy Island* cranks up and Sansaray snickers back the dead bolt and comes back over to the bed, while the doorknob on the door slowly turns, while the door slowly opens, while the door slowly opens all the way for Dacey, for Dace, for the pumped-up, veined-up spook of a Dacey spook wearing *whites,* wearing Universal Security Service *whites,* Universal Security Service *white* gloves, Universal Security Service *white* pants, a Universal Security Service *white* shirt with the Universal Security Service patch on the sleeve; and from what I can see from standing with my Shadow Security *gray* pants and my Shadow Security *gray* skivvies down around the tops of my Shadow Security boots, out behind Dacey is Pussy Galore and the DinoSores, and out behind Pussy Galore and the DinoSores are Pussy Galore's roadies, and lined up and stretching out behind the roadies are the kid-little-cuntlets with their rock-and-roll look, and behind the kid-little-cuntlets are the men and women of Shadow Security, and from what I can see from standing where I am standing, out behind the Shadow Security men and women is a pizza delivery man fucking naked from the waist down, naked with his little hairy woman-bait standing out like a shroom, and behind the pizza delivery man is a man standing with his legs crossed, and lined up behind that man is Sansaray's father, Sansaray's mother, her grandmother, her four sisters, her brother Levon, and behind her brother Levon is a man, no make that a woman, a woman that is—my God—that woman is my wife—when Sansaray, spreading herself, spreading her vajaguar wide, says, "Now, lover, eat now."

THE REPORTER

"Jesus wept" is the way Jim puts it.

"Jesus wept, all right," is the way Paley puts it. Paley puts it the way Paley puts it while waiting for Jim. Jim types his obit. Jim cranks the sheet of paper out of the typewriter. Jim stacks the sheet of paper with the other sheets of paper. Jim hands the paper to Paley. Paley reads out loud.

James Peter Kittridge today joined the do-it-yourselfer club. Membership, as far as he knew, was a family first. The father he never knew, he was told, pneumonia-wheezed his last. The mother and two older sisters died from cancers and kidneys and hearts too big. The mother and two sisters he knew best rose in the dark and the cold of that mill town. They walked the nearly four miles to work. They worked twelve hours in the roar of the looms. They walked the nearly four miles back. Home was the flapping of shirts frozen between tenements. Home was waiting in the dark for their coming home. When they came home, there was the light and the stirring of the potato soup. There was the reading of the Bible out loud while they ate. There was the threading of the rosaries in bed. There was the dying in bed. There was the dying under the gaze of Jesus.

A kind of living was had from the freights along

that mill town siding. That, and shouldering beef. That, and stacking cinder block. That, and finding a man as good as a good man. The good man put him to work pasting up, running copy, setting type. When none of the others were around to send, the good man sent him. He crossed the ice of the pond. He bellied to where the hunter clawed black water. He held on to the hunter and prayed. Dusk seeped over the cornfield. Dusk seeped over the pond. He held on and prayed, until the others came running down through the corn-stubbled dark.

After that, the good man showed him. He typed with two fingers while the good man said, "Jesus wept. Got it? Try again."

There was trying on the four-alarm fire so hot he heard the teeth popping of those trapped inside. There was the four-year-old found at the dump. There was the driver headless after driving into a tree.

When the war came in four-inch headlines, he jumped from airplanes at night. He watched for Arabs standing on high ground. He learned how it was to be afraid for so long.

Back from the war, he learned to think of his wounds, once they scabbed over brown and hard, as medals bestowed for living. Back all the way was living with his wife-to-be and her two daughters. That, and the wedding. That, and the sleeping with his medaled leg between the legs of his wife.

Given time, there was the sleeplessness. There was the trying day after day in the name of Jesus.

There were the cancers and kidneys. There was the wanting to-do-it himself. The wanting grew, indifferent to family and prayer and trying again. The wanting grew, until the wanting was all that was left. That, and the question when.

Older versions of himself could be found most nights at the end of the bar, in the column three times a week, in all the usual lies. He lied that he was doing some good. He lied that he had given back all that he was given. The truth was, he was tired of lying.

He typed his obit.

He drove to where they lived.

He looked in on his wife sleeping.

He took the Colt from the desk.

He waited.

He waited in the dark, until knowing no one was coming.

"Nope" is the way Paley puts it. Paley puts it the way Paley puts it while handing back the paper. "Nope, and it is going to stay nope until you get it right. Got it?"

Jim laughs.

"That son-of-a-bitch laughed" is the way Paley later put it.

WAYS OF SEEING

Who of us trusts his own way of seeing?

For instance, from where he whomped down on the water mattress, Bolio can see past the drunken faces. Bolio sees past the insect-charged halo of the parking lot lights to the sky and a few summer stars. As a boy, Bolio imagined the stars were pinholes in the painted-Easter-eggshell-dome of Heaven letting in the light from a room pale and bare except for the egg-enclosed universe and a huge sun bulb. Now, for the first time in a long time, Bolio again imagines seeing the stars as such, one of his few inventions, while seeing the gacked-up faces surrounding him, the owner hustling over with the tape measure. Moving anything other than his head would disqualify the toss. Bolio raises only his head and eyeball estimates twenty-two feet, five inches.

"I would say twenty-four feet, four inches," says the owner of this tavern.

The owner runs the tape measure from the foul line to Bolio's closest body part, which, for this toss, is the second toe of his right foot. On both of Bolio's feet, the second toe is bigger than the big toe.

"Mark that twenty-four feet, six inches," the owner says, drawing applause, huzzahs from the whooped-up young.

Lifted from the water mattress to his outsized feet, Bolio runs back to Ermack. Bolio lies on the mat at Ermack's feet. The mat is the same kind of mat you knew in high school or junior high school gym. Remember those mats? Remember what looks like horsehair stuffing sticking out? Remember when you were next to somersault or cartwheel and you were not ready? Remember feeling you would never be ready? Remember feeling the sweat roll down your ribs?

"Are you ready, Bolio?" Ermack asks.

From down on the mat, Bolio can see Ermack's white high tops with the looping purple laces. Bolio can see Ermack's mismatched tube socks stretching over freckled calves.

"Yes," Bolio lies, raising an arm and a leg.

Bolio closes his eyes as Ermack grabs Bolio's upraised wrist and ankle. Bolio listens.

"Errr-mack! Errr-mack! Errr-mack!" the crowd chants.

Ermack's lift shifts into crow hop, spin, launch as he slings Bolio skyward. Bolio sees spinning stars and meteor showers riddling the black eggshell dome of his eyelids.

Ermack's best invention may be Ermack.

"My eyes are as piercing as coat-hanger darts tufted with cotton balls lung heaved from a glass blowgun," Ermack says.

"My breath is the exhaust from a fifty-five Caddie doing eighty on open road," Ermack says.

"My will is a pack of starving dogs let loose in a butcher shop," Ermack says.

"My heart is the sound of the late night train moving

through the town and sleep of your childhood," Ermack says.

"My mind is a boomerang to throw farther and farther until I am afraid it will not come back, and then, when it does, I throw it again," Ermack says.

Ermack has his invention while Bolio has his feet. Bolio's feet are too long and too big for his three-foot, seven-inch length. Bolio's feet are too big for his ninety-eight-pound body.

"Your long toes with the second toes bigger than the big toes is where you began," Ermack says.

"All that egg-growth spurted down to your feet, exploded down to your toes in an all-out effort to make you big, bigger," Ermack says.

Ermack may be right, Bolio thinks. Maybe Bolio began with his feet, Bolio thinks. Maybe Bolio ends at his feet. When Bolio cums, that electric-urge twitches down his little legs to arc and sputter in his big feet.

"A zillion little Bolios turning cold on your belly," Ermack says.

"A zillion little protozoan Bolios with big heads and big hands and big feet somersaulting in your Milky Way spill," Ermack says.

Walking to the tavern, Bolio sees many of the same young cruising up and down the strip.

"The same young faces cruise up and down this strip like pharaohs on the Nile," Ermack says.

"At the same time, youth to the young seems shuffling, barely able," Ermack says.

"Youth is a tyrant, a small tyrant to the young, a large tyrant to the old," Ermack says.

"The young are like you, Bolio, with your body a tyrant to your mind," Ermack says.

Ermack may be right, and yet, Ermack has plenty of youth cruising for him.

"My joy is winter light snapping off a fast-moving stream," Ermack says.

"My anger is the anger of a whore, cold and sad," Ermack says.

"My arrogance is the arrogance of dreams," Ermack says.

"My past is the town where you grew up, which is now just somewhere on the way to somewhere else," Ermack says.

"My present is returning home from a cold night to the warmth of a sleeping child you love," Ermack says.

"My future is a too short fucking drive over a fast new road," Ermack says.

When you get this low you really get to see the summer sky.

"Are you ready, Bolio?" Ermack asks.

Bolio raises his head and sees the faces of the young. Bolio sees the owner ready with the tape measure for Ermack's last toss. Ermack needs a toss of more than twenty-eight feet, five inches to win tonight.

"Yes," Bolio lies, raising his arm and leg starward.

"No, Bolio," Ermack says.

"Something new, Bolio," Ermack says, his face souped-up with all his youth, all his will.

"On your back, Bolio," Ermack says. "Roll on your back and cross your arms like so."

Bolio rolls on his back and crosses his arms. Ermack takes hold of Bolio's feet.

"Not my feet," Bolio says.

"Yes, Bolio," Ermack says. "You will see."

Bolio closes his eyes. Bolio listens.

"Errr-mack! Errr-mack! Errr-mack!"

Ermack's lift glides to spin, another spin, snap as he boomerangs Bolio nightward.

Bolio spins over the upraised faces, over the thirty-foot mark, out over the water mattress. Bolio spins in the stars squint-seen as a sieve of light slanting, cartwheeling, exploding. Bolio spins on until seeing, finally, how suited the heart is for this life's ride.

FLAMINGOS AND OTHER SELF-CURES, ALMOST

I knew something was needed so I planted one on top of Zio Frank. It was hard finding something that spoke to me. Once found, the something was harder to steal. I am talking one of these Day-Glo plastic flamingos with a black hook of a beak and a neck like a question mark. The neck curves down to a molded hollow body and folded black-tipped wings. The legs are two-foot-long wire rods sticking into underbelly bearing the words MADE IN LEOMINSTER, MASS. I am talking simple and complete, ready to plant when and where you want. I planted one on top of Zio Frank.

Mornings I am not buzzed I go out driving around. Driving around, seeing what is available, is something we used to do. We meaning me and Zio Frank. It is how I found the flamingo. It is how I spend my mornings. I get behind the wheel of Zio Frank's big Impala, one of the old ones with the manta-ray fins and roomy, you forget how roomy, interior. Since my butt has come to resemble gnawed pig knuckle, I get behind the wheel of the Impala as carefully as I can. What hurts most is knowing how Elaine, Zio Frank's wife, my aunt, will call the cops if she catches me. She has already. She has promised to do so again. I wait until she goes to dancercize class to schmooze and wiggle her wide butt—no pig knuckle there—schmooze and wiggle between the hours of ten and two Monday through Friday. I wait until she goes to class before flashing the spare key she does not know about. I inch my tender, runny butt behind the wheel. I sit until I am used to the pain again. I sit smelling Zio Frank's smell, his brand of smokes and after-shave. I sit until I am used to the pain again before sliding down, sliding slowly down until as little of the raw as possible is left on the front seat. I slide down until I can barely see over the dash.

Half sitting, half lying down, I start up the big Impala and ease it down the driveway. I ease the Impala faster along the back roads and through the spreading subdivisions. The Impala almost seems to take over, leaving me in my butt-chewed-way to see what is available. Available is his word, Zio Frank's word. Driving around, seeing what is available, was his big thing, the thing that almost cured him. I said almost. The flamingo is mine.

Most of the time you have to cure yourself. This is true, is it not? Zio Frank tried. He tried to cure himself of a lot of things. It beat hell out of coming home from the plumbing and machine shop the way he did: the same plumbing and machine shop he worked at thirty-six years: coming home all private and sulky and stay out of my way. Nights he came home like this, the first thing he did was galumph sulky and pissed-off to the fridge. This and hook back a cold longneck and roll his eyes up until they looked like the eyeholes in a mask. This and blow out as if he just surfaced from the cold, cold bottom of a lake. All this paved the way for the rest of the night: a night in his easy chair smoking and killing a six of longnecks and watching TV: a night of watching the same news over and over followed by comedy shows where the women are jiggle and shriek. All this sitting and smoking and killing and watching pretty well poleaxed him, put him under until the smoke between his fingers burned down to the knuckles. Other than sulk there was no complaint, not to me, so I can only guess he was worn down working through the morning, through the day, through the thirty-six years: worn down working just to pay the bills: worn down watching TV and waking up with knuckles on fire until it was either do something different or die. The truth is he did both, and the way he began was by driving around seeing what else was available.

Me, I drive around because I am not smart enough to think of anything else; getting buzzed takes no genius. Mornings I am not buzzed I go out driving around.

I drove almost two weeks' worth of sober mornings before finding the Day-Glo. It was hard. It took me two weeks to see beyond the usual. I am talking the usual gas-fed barbecues, wishing wells, and such. None of the usual spoke to me, so I drove more. I drove until I saw something that spoke to me, something as in lawn jockeys, lawn jockeys both white and black. I am talking concrete lawn jockeys with caps and painted silks and knee-high black boots: the ones holding lanterns as if looking for someone or something. This is what spoke to me, this meaning the looking part. That is until getting close and really seeing the look. Both lawn jockey races, white and black, have the same look. Look closely next time you see a lawn jockey and you will see what I mean. It is a baring of teeth and it spooks me. It spooks me in that it reminds me of when I could look in the rearview. Before my butt was chewed and I could look in the rearview, this look was the same as mine.

When Zio Frank began, he began big. I am talking big and then some. I am talking life-size. I am talking a day or two after he started driving around seeing what is available, she appeared out behind the garage. I saw her while mowing the lawn. She is hard to miss. I said life-size. I am talking statuesque. I am talking biggest I have seen. I am talking bigger than me and when buzzed I feel almost life-size. She is, the Bathtub Virgin that is.

Standing barefoot on a half-globe base, the Bathtub Virgin is protected by an upright quarter-buried bathtub covered with concrete and strings of blue lights; the same color blue as the long concrete veil covering her head and shoulders: the same sky blue as her Heaven-raised eyes that say to me, Yes, I have known both beauty and shit.

Imagine. Imagine all this. Imagine all this and then some as in bare white feet and hands emerging from the concrete folds of a long white robe: a robe like the one Elaine, Zio Frank's wife, my aunt, sometimes wears, only with Elaine's robe you can see the outline of her nips.

As far as I can tell, and I have looked closely, the Bathtub Virgin does not have any, nips that is. She does not have any nips or tits or butt, not that I should talk, not about butts, not anymore, but the Bathtub Virgin has no butt, especially when matched against Elaine. When Elaine wears a skirt, her wide butt looks like two small dogs fighting in a bag. She was some beginning, the Bathtub Virgin that is. Elaine came later.

Me, I took my time. I took almost two weeks' worth of mornings easing the big Impala around the back roads and through the spreading subdivisions. Besides the usual, I saw lions and porcelain rooster planters filled with mums. I saw pipe-sucking leprechauns and ceramic donkeys on power mower chassis. None of these spoke to me, so I drove. I drove sober and it seemed a long time. I drove until something spoke to me. Something spoke to me at the Mohawk Mobile Home Adult Park, speed limit ten miles per. I drove within the speed limit around the park's roads: a grid of roads named after famous Indians and Indian tribes: Pocahontas Place, Cheyenne Way, Tecumseh Court.

On Tecumseh Court I heard. In the fenced-in yard of a small black and white mobile home I saw. I saw a flock of half a dozen Day-Glos with their lovely questing necks, their molded plastic bodies with that little event of upturned tail, their delicate wire legs. Every bird was simple and complete in a way that, well, you know. I parked. I parked the Impala out front of the small black and white mobile home surrounded by nip-high wire-mesh fence. Two signs were on the fence: BEWARE OF DOG and THE DEMPSEYS.

I could see Mrs. Dempsey, or rather a boiled ham

face with a smoke angling out of the mouth. She was at a window of the mobile home, stiff-arming a Venetian blind. I could see the white flesh sagging at the back of her arm, flesh as white as marble set off against the meat color of her face. I could see her head juke trying to see between the Venetian blind slats. She juked while barking hammered over and over inside the mobile home. I am talking barking that meant business. I am talking barking that made me know something else besides the first something I told you about was needed.

Then there was then some, then some after the Bathtub Virgin and before Elaine. I am talking Zio Frank driving around, seeing what is available. I am talking Zio Frank driving around before work as well as after work. I am talking Zio Frank driving around and seeing and then some, then some as in patio. I am talking marble patio.

"The best that is available," Zio Frank said; Zio Frank, who once came home from the plumbing and machine shop all private and sulky and stay out of my way. I am talking once, once in that he quit. He quit working and sulking and took to driving around, seeing what is available, full time.

"The best that is available," Zio Frank said. He was talking patio. He was talking marble patio, midnight chill and quiet. Us sweating despite the chill. Us meaning me and Zio Frank. Us sweating while heaving marble slabs into the back seat of the Impala: marble slabs wrecking the shocks and filling the Impala's interior, you forget how roomy interior, with the smell of damp and moss: these same marble slabs now planted around our pool.

Sitting around our pool killing longnecks you can read as in JASON COCKBURN or LUCILLE ASHTON 1846–1902 or JOHN CHILSON BELOVED BROTHER AND DEVOTED SON. You can read all this, all this and then some.

The flamingos and Mrs. Dempsey can keep a while longer. Let us talk Elaine, Zio Frank's wife, my aunt: the same Elaine who called the cops on me and said she will do so again: the same Elaine who until a short time ago was not Zio Frank's wife, was not my aunt: the same Elaine I first met while mowing the lawn around our marble patio and pool. She said Frank said come over any time and use the pool. She came over. She came over more.

I did not mind her coming over, not even with her wide no-pig-knuckle butt, not that I should talk, not anymore, not about butts, but I did not mind, even with her wide butt she can barely keep in her zebra-striped bikini: more butt than bikini, more butt and then some. I am talking low rider. I am talking varicose veins. I am talking fleshy butt.

As soft and as wide and as fleshy as Elaine is you know where, her face is hard. It is hard in a way you might think stupid. It is not. It is not unkind either, even after calling the cops on me. It is a face with a slash of red lipstick and eyes that look at me like she knows I would not mind sticking whatever instinct I own between those red lipsticked lips.

I guess Zio Frank felt the same way. He said come over any time. She came over. She came over more. She stayed. They married.

While killing longnecks and watching some jiggle and shriek, I could sometimes hear them upstairs. I could hear them going at it with all the wherewithal lips and mouths and bellies and whatever else can muster. When Zio Frank did, muster that is, I could hear him moan like he was gut shot.

I am talking Tecumseh Court again. I am talking looking at the imprisoned flock and listening to the barking and knowing: knowing something was needed: knowing I needed something else to get that first something. I am talking just one and not a longneck, not my well-known mean drunk act either, not my stay too long and fall down thing, not my sick dog stuff. I am talking none of that, well, almost none of that, and just one. Knowing what I knew, I opened the door of the Impala and got out. Mrs. Dempsey of THE DEMPSEYS, meat face at the window, left the blind to appear at the mobile home's screen door. A dog, a barking silhouette of doggy fury, appeared with her.

"Is this the Dempsey residence?" I asked.

Mrs. Dempsey stared while the dog boomed his voice around the inside of the mobile home and bounced himself off the screen door Mrs. Dempsey kept closed with both white-as-marble arms.

"Is the mister in?" I asked, pitching my voice down like a fat TV detective.

The woman and the dog stared more; she with smoke curling around that face; the dog with ears raised.

"No need to worry, ma'am," I said. "I am here to tell you there have been reports of high levels of radiation found in some lawn ornaments, especially flamingos. Don't worry, ma'am, not yet, but I do have to look at your flock."

I said what I said while closing the gate behind me, while trying not to step in the dog's huge shit piles. It was useless, the shit piles were huge and all over.

I thought of the Bathtub Virgin. I thought of her covered with concrete and strings of blue lights, the same sky blue as her Heaven-raised eyes. I thought of the Bathtub Virgin and, this is the truth, got down on my knees in the shit piles and crawled all around and made a little show of looking at each flamingo.

By the time I crawled all around, going so far as taking a pad out of my back pocket and pretending to take notes, by the time I crawled all around to the last flamingo smaller and more Day-Glo than the others, I knew.

"I will have to take this one in," I said, meaning the one slightly smaller and more Day-Glo than the other ones.

"I am talking about having to take this one in now," I said, getting to my feet. As I lifted the plastic bird off its wire legs, Mrs. Dempsey swung open the screen door.

Zio Frank got his walking their bed. I was downstairs killing and watching some more you know what when instead of a moan, a moan like I told you about, I heard a cough. Zio Frank coughed like somebody trying to swallow a fleshy hairball.

Elaine, her hard face even harder in her seriousness, padded naked into the living room. She came downstairs serious and naked and rippling and butt and said call an ambulance. When the ambulance arrived, Zio Frank's eyes were open, but he was not awake.

Me, I felt sleepy with fear. Mrs. Dempsey swung open the screen door and I asked myself whether I was too sleepy to try. I was not too sleepy to try, and made it out the gate and almost halfway across Tecumseh Court. I was almost halfway, when I turned and saw the white in the muzzle. I saw the white and how one of the eyelids was torn off showing a white ball looking straight up. The other eye was red and big as a big dog's eye. I looked into that eye and knew that I was a doomed pretender.

Me on my knees on the examining table in the emergency room. Me more hurt and bloody than I knew.

"This looks like pig knuckle," the doctor said while tweezing away strips of bloody underwear and blue jean. He tweezed away while I passed out of me.

When I came to, and this is something, I felt pretty good. But for the pain in my butt, I felt pretty good. What I mean is, but for the pain, I felt as pretty good as I can ever remember feeling.

I felt pretty good right up to when the cops stopped

by: the same cops Elaine, Zio Frank's wife, my aunt, called. The cops stopped by and we talked. We talked Impala. We talked bloody front seat. We talked flamingo and all. We talked and I lied. The cops laughed and told me unlicensed, unregistered and uninsured use of a motor vehicle.

Elaine's, Zio Frank's wife's, my aunt's unauthorized use charge was dropped after I told her I would not take the Impala out again until all this was straightened out. I lied to her too. You know. You know mornings I am not buzzed I go out driving around between the hours of ten and two. Mornings I am not buzzed, and it has been almost six weeks' worth now, I go out driving around. Six weeks and I still know. I still know so I inch my tender, runny butt behind the wheel and go out driving around, seeing what is available.

Sometimes I stop by and see Zio Frank and the flamingo. The flamingo is a little unsteady on TV antenna wire legs: a little unsteady so I lean the flamingo against Zio Frank's half-ton marble marker: a marble marker I know nothing short of four-wheel drive and winch will move.

This is not all I know. I know this is no cure, but maybe it is a beginning, maybe even a beginning and then some.

DEAR TO
WHOEVER FINDS THIS
AND READS THIS SO
THAT YOU SHOULD
KNOW DOZIER AND
ME ARE NOT ALL
BAD, AT LEASTWISE
NOT DOZIER

Anything can happen now that everything has.

Don't you wish it is you who says this? I wish it is me who says this, only it is Dozier who says this. I cannot think of a single anything to say since writing this down is not my idea in the first place and is Dozier's idea, with Dozier saying to me, LaDonna darling, be my writing-down angel and write all this down like you are an angel come to earth. Some angel I am, not even knowing what to write down first. I say to Dozier, What should I write down first? Dozier does not say anything, only is keeping his hands on the steering wheel and is keeping his eyes straight ahead on the road with the bugs shooting white out from the black from the both sides of the road like they are shooting at us. I wonder maybe Dozier is thinking about the same what I am thinking about and is not hearing me, only Dozier hears me all right, for after I watch the bugs shoot out some more and after I nearly quit thinking what I was thinking about I told you about, and after I start getting asleepier and asleepier, which is the why this writing is slanting down now the way it is slanting down, Dozier says to me, LaDonna darling, write this, write anything can happen now that everything has. As you can see, I wrote this down and also write what I just wrote.

· · ·

This is maybe not what Dozier had in mind when he asked me to be his writing-down angel, only Dozier is the only this I can think of right now to write down about. This is Dozier road mapped out for you as Dozier is right now, starting with the nothing Dozier has on what he calls his mechanic tan southernmosts. Take Dozier's closest bare southernmost, the one on the gas pedal, and jump your mind up from the toe traffic jam to the squiggly green veins under what was Dozier's inside-all-day skin as if somebody started squiggly drawing a road map using his skin and a green crayon to draw with. The little squiggle of highway goes in under the underside of anklebone before starting up again to spread out from the higher-up muscle bunch of down under Dozier. From the bunch of muscle-up, the in and out of vein gets bigger, at leastwise looks bigger, gets to be what could be interstates shooting up to the outside of what could be a side of the road rest stop on top of Dozier's old baldy knee worn bald by the rubbing of Dozier's jeans when Dozier is wearing jeans, only now Dozier is wearing baggy army cutoffs and a T. From under the sleeves of Dozier's T, the big seeable, what I call interstates, start up again, bulk squiggling out again at the big humped-out arm muscle half mechanic tanned and half sunburned. These interstates squiggly dip down, up, into the nearly all sunburned before becoming four-lane divided dividing out into the crowded underside of elbow to wrist before tunneling under Dozier's watchband. The back of Dozier's sunburned hand, the one on the steering wheel, has the veins forking out and running over themselves into a kind of downtown busyness ending with Dozier's fingernails rimmed in tarred parking lot black. Next comes Dozier's scenic overlook, starting with the sunburn riding up his neck to his clean-shaven unpaved Dozier says he shaves every other day for me. Next comes Dozier's wooded parkland of curly black hair that if you were me you would not mind camping out in and maybe getting lost in. Talking about getting lost in, Dozier's toll-limited lips let me in in a way that I never wanted in before and do not want out of until what is the innermost of me is tongue driving around down inside Dozier, driving down Dozier's throat and down inside Dozier until I am looking out Dozier's eyes at what is the outermost of me writing all this down.

Already the everything that happened seems so long ago, although in trying to figure back I guess it was only, if today is already Friday, was only Tuesday, Wednesday, Thursday, three days ago. Three days and another me, or so it seems ago, when the me that is me now awoke up out of myself asleep walking through my life in a way I did not even know about until the everything that happened to us happened. Maybe you know what I mean? Maybe something has happened to you to all of a sudden make you say to yourself, Where have I been until now? How did I get anything done until now? How did I get to where I am now? Three days and a lifetime ago and here I am now with the heat rising wrinkly off the road the way it is and whip-shaking the hair on the off sides of our heads the way it is and sucking in hot over us the way it is and sticking us to these seats the way it is so every time one of us moves it sounds like somebody tearing tape. This wrinkly and this whip-shaking straight and this sucking in hot and this tearing tape of our skin means I am wide awake, at leastwise I think I am wide awake, although the truth is it does seem a little like dreaming with Dozier riding us to the anything that can happen next.

All the what Dozier is about on the outside I road mapped out for you is one thing. All the what Dozier is about on the inside is another thing. What Dozier is on the inside is not as easy to write down about as the what on the outside, not that that was easy, only with me, what you see, which is not much, is what you get. With Dozier, what you see, at leastwise what you see on the outside, seems a whole lot different than what is on the inside. On the outside, Dozier looks like he can take care of himself and anybody and anything else needing to be taken care of. On the inside, Dozier is . . . Dozier. What this girl is trying to say to you the best I know how, which I know is none too good, is that inside of Dozier, in spite of what you might first think on first seeing Dozier, and in spite of what Dozier did or does, is a lot of something making somebody like me want to do for Dozier the best I can. At the same time, something else in me wants to say I most likely will never be able to do for Dozier, at leastwise not in the way Dozier most wants, whatever that way is. Maybe this is true for all of us and those we love the most.

· · ·

This is written down in the dark with Dozier having us
settled in on sixty, only with the dark the way the dark
is, you, dear whoever you are reading this, will have to
forgive me if this writing down is not on the lines and
is all over instead, only I have to write down to you
now so you should know to forget about most of the
whatever you might hear about what Dozier and me
did or did not do and about the everything that did or
did not happen. The truth is, who other than Dozier
and me and maybe Stepdaddy really cares about the
everything that happened? More of the truth is but for
Stepdaddy's seventy-three-and-whatever-the-change-
was, I bet, and maybe you can hear Dozier doing the
talking and me trying to pass it off a little that it is me
doing the talking, only we bet Stepdaddy does not really
care much about what happened. Everybody we meet
seems to only care about and is only talking about this
weather, talking this sit-on-you heat and how no end to
the heat is in sight. To tell you the truth some more,
sometimes Dozier starts the weather talk himself by saying in his best-natured-Dozier way, Lots of weather
we're having lately. Dozier says you can tell a lot about
a person from the way they answer that, if they bother
answering. Knowing this, I say to you whatever you
likely hear about Dozier and me and about what Dozier
and me did or did not do and about the everything that
did or did not happen is not worth knowing much about
and just is.

Dozier believes in getting up early, getting up either
with first light or a little before to see the sun light up

as far as you can see. Dozier says there is something about that light and about that time of day that gives a someone a kind of hope, a kind of promise of what the day might bring. I say let me asleep, although the only time I have ever gotten up that early, at leastwise after awhile after the only one time I have ever gotten up that early, there was, and there most likely still is, if I could only get up, all the not having to go anywhere we do not want to go, or do anything we do not want to do, and if we want we can spend the whole day out of this heat somewhere, stopping out at some spinachy sump hole somewhere to laze around in the choked-off shallows talking about what we want and what we will do and where we will go, or if we want we can go, go five hundred miles north, south, east, west to see some of the nearly everything I have never seen and most likely will never see again. Along with all of Dozier himself, all this is nearly enough to make me maybe think Dozier is right about what Dozier says about getting up with first light.

This is again maybe not what Dozier most likely had in mind for me to write down about when he asked me to be his writing-down angel, so this will be just between you and me, not that you might likely will want any of it anywhere near you once you know what it is. It can happen anywhere at any time just like it happened now with Dozier cruising Dozier and me who cares where with my hand cramping up with my writing all this down when Dozier gets his little look to himself like Dozier is amusing himself, not as if there is anything bad about amusing yourself, or even so bad about Dozier's little look to himself so much as what comes after his little look. What comes after his little look is a kind of bark or a string of barks, and I do not mean a kind of bark the same as the bulldog's bark so much as a ripping-out-fast bark followed by Dozier saying, Uh-oh, trouser mice, or Uh-oh, listen to these trouser mice barking it up. Dozier's saying what he says is not as bad as what Dozier does next, especially in this heat sticking us to these seats as it is already and sweating us through what little we have on. After Dozier does what he does, Dozier says, LaDonna darling, I know these trouser mice are loud, only don't you know the louder the better since the louder ones don't smell as bad as the softer ones smell. When this does not work Dozier says, LaDonna, between you and me, darling, trouser mice between a man and a woman is the highest kind of closeness. When this does not work either, Dozier says, LaDonna honey, do you think I would do this if I did not want to share with you the all of me there is to share, both the good and the bad all of me. Only trouser mice are somehow not what I had in mind when Dozier long ago already said to me, Are you coming? I am coming and going and trying to write all this down the best I can and trying to love Dozier, the all of Dozier, the all of the good and the all of the bad of Dozier the best I can.

You are always in more shit than you think you are in.

You can guess who it is who says this and you can also guess the other who it is who wishes she does not

have to say this, only now does have to say this. You
remember what I wrote you about hearing about the
what seemed like the everything Dozier and me did that
really seemed like everything, and in some ways was,
only with nobody but Dozier and me and maybe Stepdaddy really caring? Now some others care about what
happens and about what Dozier and me do or do not
do. I do not mean the same some others as maybe you
who might have been wondering all along now how we
have been getting along asleeping and eating. The answer to your wondering is we have been getting along better than all right, asleeping in the back or on the roof
of the van and eating wherever we can find salad bars
where you most likely already know you can fill up a
tray all glopped over with all the chunked-up creamy
that you could want. Anyway, to make a short story
shorter, seventy-three-and-whatever-the-change-was, as
much money as this is, was, does not go as far as you
might think, even asleeping in the van and eating
glopped-over salad sometimes three times a day. To tell
you the truth some more, even with our doing all what
we are doing, I did not think much about where the
seventy-three-and-whatever-the-change-was was going,
even when we pulled up at one of these self-serves. This
self-serve is run by a fat guy so fat it makes you wonder
about laying off the chunked-up creamy, not that I have
anything against fat guys or fat anyones or fat any-
things, at leastwise not that I know that I do, only this
fat guy is so fat sitting inside the little glassed-in and
cinder-blocked self-serve with all the ciggies and with
all the candy bars and with the little TV on and with
his two big fans blowing right on all his fat, that it has

to make you wonder. Now this fat guy, although I suppose it is not his fault he is fat, is so fat that just sitting and not doing anything other than just sitting is enough to make his fat tremble. This fat guy with his fat trembles more when his fat-guy hand and his fat-guy fingers push out the spring-loaded drawer at Dozier with Dozier putting in a five and saying, Hidy, lots of weather we're having lately. This fat guy, with even his hair slicked straight back looking fat, trembles around the lower half of his face with the word *regular* coming out. Dozier is not saying anything until I start wondering maybe Dozier is not hearing the fat guy, only Dozier is hearing the fat guy all right with Dozier saying, Regular, along with this lady, meaning me, would like to use your dumper. This fat guy, fat lips, fat chin, fat everything I can see gone trembling to fat says, There is a faucet out back. Dozier says, This lady, meaning me, don't need to use a faucet, if you know what I mean. The fat guy trembles back how the faucet out back is all there is to use. Dozier says, Then what do YOU use when YOU have to use the dumper? Before the fat guy can say something back for me to hear, I am on my way out back to over near where the faucet is where nobody if they were around could really see me anyway, and squat down with my sun dress up in my arm crooks and watch the trickle thread itself out through the dust before skinning over to a stop. I try twisting the faucet on, only this faucet has not been used in awhile, or if it has been used, whoever used it last really twisted the faucet off tight. Using both hands I cannot even start twisting the faucet on. I go back around to tell Dozier watching the PAY THIS AMOUNT

93

rolling up, and tell him, when Dozier says all short, You do this! I am doing the pumping with Dozier sticky popping over the hot sticky tar over to the glassed-in fat guy again when I notice besides the sticky popping of Dozier's flip-flops, that Dozier has the bulldog stuck barrel down and mostly hanging out of the back pocket of Dozier's cutoffs drooping way low down in back. The PAY THIS AMOUNT starts slowing down some with me clicking and squeezing out every last all what I can. I only half hear Dozier say something to the cinder-blocked and glassed-in fat guy about how YOU, meaning the fat guy, really better take a look, when I half see the fat guy take his fat old time tremble heave himself off whatever he is sitting on and tremble huff himself the way really fat guys do over to the door and let himself out with a key and with the same key lock the door behind him when Dozier has the bulldog out. The fat guy, tremble huffing and rolling from side to side the way really fat guys do, looks back and sees Dozier has the bulldog out. I look around and see nobody else around, only me and Dozier and the fat guy unlocking the door again, only this time to let in himself and Dozier. I clank up the nozzle seven cents over and twist on the cap and go around and get in. In the little glassed-over, and with the way Dozier and the fat guy seem to be moving so slow, they look to me as if they are moving underwater. Dozier and the fat guy look to me as if they are talking underwater with me not able to hear what they are talking about, only I bet it is not the weather, only with Dozier you never really know. They are talking with the fat guy doing most of the talking when Dozier, just as slow and as calm as Dozier can be, blaps the fat guy a slow one with the bulldog. Something black starts slow down the fat guy's no longer-combed-straight-back fat-looking hair and the fat guy is doing something slow and underwater with his hands I cannot see, while as calm as can be, as slow as can be, Dozier is slow stuffing, with his hand not holding the bulldog, something into the pockets of his bagging-out cutoffs. Dozier stops his slow underwater stuffing and, as easygoing as Dozier gets, backs out the door. The hand not holding the bulldog is in Dozier's pocket while the other hand is dangling, pointing the bulldog down at the sitting-down fat guy. I can only say pointing though I am seeing this all the while and not seeing or hearing the bulldog go off once, never mind the twice the newspaper says, only I did see the fat guy all of a sudden look up at Dozier in a way I knew the fat guy knew that whatever much shit he thought he was in before, that he was in a lot more shit now.

The feeling of having just awoke up out of myself that seems long ago already, and is long ago already, grows dreamier and dreamier with this going and going and with this fun-house-mirror-making-everything heat and with this knowing heavy up inside me now that the some others, whoever they are, are coming. Dozier says the some others are not the same some others I most likely think they are, and how they always come for you with smiles, and how they always come for you as friends, and how they always come for you at a time when you are at your weakest. Dozier says the only what we can do is keep doing what we are doing, keep going and going, keep trying to get around this heat, keep the bulldog wrapped up in the greasy rag on the seat between us, keep writing all this down to keep the feeling of having just awoke up out of ourselves from getting away from ourselves.

This is us, Dozier and me, and the more that is the us together and how most nights we try and get around this heat lay-over-your-face hot. This is the more that is us, with nothing other than a few jacks around and with nobody we know of around and with nothing on, other than sweat, up on top of the van on top of Dozier's old asleeping bag. This is the more of us together, cooking in our own juices after making more than either of us alone could make. This is the bigger us, cooking and watching off at the thin wires of lightning lighting up the clouds and the dark. Down below us, Dozier has the game on the radio with the talk of whoever that is talking now as almost close as somebody you have known a long time, an uncle on your mama's side you love and you see once a year and has come to visit now and is in the room next to your room talking low. This is all of us, cooking through Dozier's old asleeping bag with this all-over-us heat, only with all our cooking through, only with all the more that is the us together, there is still not enough us for me with me wanting and with me having Dozier's arm and Dozier's hand around and over and on me. This is me, tracing down from Dozier's snugged-down watchband without seeing anything about Dozier but the what is Dozier that is in my head. This is me, blind tracing the hairs on the back of Dozier's hand to the bumped-up smooth of Dozier's crossing over and fanning out interstate off-shoots I now trace back the other way as far as I can trace back with me inside my head wanting to be inside Dozier tracing all the way around the inside of Dozier until tracing, finding, and staying forever safe in the heart of Dozier's heart.

Those some others coming for us came. Up in these hills is already cooler with the one way up hairpinning around and up past the sliders, past the snow fields, until we are in the climbed-up-coolness with either going all the way back down into the heat the same hairpinning way we came up, or going on. Those some others, two of them, are a him sitting inside collecting, and a her standing outside wearing a wide-brimmed hat and an open heavy coat the same as he is wearing, only her open heavy coat is humped up in back by a holster with her looking in the cars, nodding in and saying something in to the each of the three cars ahead, then two, then our van with the wrapped-up bulldog on the seat between us with her nodding in and looking in at Dozier with Dozier saying, Lots of weather we're having lately, and her not saying anything, only looking in at Dozier with her face having lost all her how-do. Dozier's face has his little look like he is amusing himself until her finally saying, Enough weather to suit me, with Dozier then holding out the five and the two ones and her saying to Dozier, Hand it to him, and Dozier pulling up and handing him the five and the two ones and me looking and finding one quarter, another quarter to make the fifty, and me handing the fifty to Dozier with Dozier handing the fifty to him with him saying, Thank you, and with Dozier not saying anything more, only going and going until we are gone.

Dozier and me are fat wrapped in the all we have to put on put on against this watch-yourself-smoke-out-the-inside-of-yourself cold. Dozier is still asleeping down in the tunneled-down warm of us caterpillared together down inside Dozier's old asleeping bag. That was us, until me awaking up and wriggling up and unzipping and rolling out and zipping Dozier back up. The moon was ghosting down enough for me to see by to get out this notepad and to open to this page only without me writing anything down to you without first watching the soft asleeping little hills that was and is Dozier still asleeping, watching the rest of what I can watch from up on top of the van of the lake below, of the moonlit snow, of the black of these surrounding hills that I watch until nearly all the moonlight ghosting down has all but ghosted away leaving the rounded backs of these hills rimmed with day. This is when I start writing this what I just wrote down to you with me knowing what you are most likely thinking about now and have most likely been thinking about for a long time now. I say to you do not worry the way I am no longer worried for I know no matter what happens from here on in that at least-wise Dozier has already been delivered and saved, if only because I have been Dozier's writing-down angel.

THE MAN
WHO FAILED TO
WHACK OFF

Among the LIVE GIRLS, SEE LIVE GIRLS, LIVE GIRLS HERE, he is Gramps, Casabas, Blinkers, Humpers, Jugs, Early Bird. Little and bent, he shuffles in after the eleven-to-oners, before the four-to-sixers. Going deep into pocket, he draws out four singles counted and folded.

"Four will get you two," Luis says, sliding over two brass tokens.

With tokens in shaking hand, he drags muscle and bone and brain giving way after eighty-three years to the REAL LIVE GIRLS, LIVE-ALL-LIVE-GIRLS, LIVE COLLEGE GIRLS calling, "Yo, Gramps! Bumpers! Get a load of these garbos, creamers, bonkers, congas, rib-bangers!"

The PACING LIVE GIRLS, LEANING LIVE GIRLS, SITTING LIVE GIRLS check polish on broken nails, eat beef lo-mein, squeeze pimples, call, "Yo, Jugs! Try petting these paw patties, oompapas, jemimas, pagodas, gob stoppers, flapjacks!"

Brass tokens clinking in hand, he looks at the GAZING LIVE GIRLS, BUBBLE-GUM-BUBBLE-BLOWING LIVE GIRLS, SMOKING LIVE GIRLS in red-curtained booths, waiting in lace and little else.

"Come on, Gramps! You ain't got forever! Get yourself some fresh chimichangas, balboas, chihuahuas, sweet rolls, sweater meat!"

In this staring time, take-as-long-as-you-want-just-hurry-it-up-time, honey-I-could-use-your-token-time, he looks for her, the ONE LIVE GIRL, the ONE PARTICULAR LIVE GIRL, the ONE-AND-ONLY-THIS-ONE LIVE GIRL named Misty, named Ginger, named Brandy, named whatever he wants to name her.

The other LIVE-AND-KICKING GIRLS, GET YOUR LIVE GIRLS, LIVE GIRLS RIGHT HERE RIGHT NOW see their chance, take the chance.

"She's working, Gramps, so try these hush puppies on for size, these peepers, wahwahs, wobblers, umlauts."

Counting his brass tokens, he smells his own smell sucked into lungs, sees the line of light under the door of the booth she uses, sees the door open to the ONE LIVE GIRL, ONE SPECIAL LIVE GIRL, ONE-AND-ONLY-THIS-ONE LIVE GIRL saying to him, "Hey, Gramps, howse it hanging?"

In the closeness of the booth where his bony narrowness is almost too big, he waits. Knowing the quickness of two minutes, of eighty-three years, he unbuttons, unzips, lets his pants fall to the sticky floor.

The clinking down of brass token becomes shade rolling up: becomes legs of a high stool: becomes dirty soles of open-toed heels on the other side of the glass: becomes stockinged legs: becomes shaved pussy flaps: becomes smooth jump of white belly: becomes breasts covered up by hands: becomes the ONE-LIVE GIRL, the BEST LIVE GIRL, the IF-YOU'VE-GOT-THE-

MONEY-I'VE-GOT-THE-TIME-HONEY-LIVE-
GIRL.

In the heat raising sweat on his brow, above his lip, under his arms, through his shirt, he holds both hands around his nodding cock as if in prayer.

The ONE LIVE GIRL, THIS ONE REAL LIVE GIRL, THIS ALWAYS THE SAME ONE LIVE GIRL helps him with, "Come on, Gramps! Come on, Grampers!"

Mouth-breathing the heat, he tries. The shade unwinds as he pumps faster, as he drops the brass token. Reaching for the token becomes stabbing behind eye: becomes dizziness: becomes sitting down hard: becomes sucking the ammonia smell: becomes sucking the cool floor: becomes suck, suck, suck.

Among the LIVE GIRLS, REAL LIVE GIRLS, LIVE GIRLS HERE is another old man who is gagas, twofers, twangers, floaters, goners.

INDIA, WHEN YOUR
PHONE DOESN'T RING,
IT'S ME, POMP

It is thoughts of her doing the everyday that sets Pomp off.

It is Pomp, small-town lawyer, one-time Baptist, volunteer fire fighter, pork-and-beaner until the day I die whose insides seize up into a morning-after when walking into the bank or the hardware store or the wherever and seeing someone with hair like her hair.

Yes, it is Pomp picking his nose meat in the checkout line at the all-night Stop & Rob while football cradling a box of chocolate-covered donuts and reading through one of these newspapers, this one newspaper with the headline: I WANT BIGFOOT'S BABY, and me wanting her to have my baby.

Back at the house, it is the same old Pomp staring in the toothpaste-spotted mirror at the same old face belonging to a middling, small-town bachelor with dark quarter moons under his eyes and a mustache that looks pasted on crooked.

It is Pomp staring back at Pomp that leads him wandering back, crawling back around to the what was, to the her, to the let us say, yes, it was true, to the her washing her face in this same spotted mirror.

Her face was as wondrous as her name.

India. India Early.

Not bad, huh?

You bet your bung-foddered patoot not bad. Her face and the rest of her were just as wondrous: the long tallness of her, the tangle of dark hair lifting out behind her when she walked, the forgiving heart, unlike my heart.

Now not-so-good old Pomp says a lot of things, but Pomp was as there with her with his heart as he was ever anywhere. Pomp saw her wondrous beauty and the rest of her stop the half-gone party goings-on. You say beauty is no guarantee of happiness. Pomp says back to you, I know, but it is something. Think of yourself at a party full of people like me putting what we think are our most charming mustached faces and the rest of our charming middling selves forward. Think of India coming into the room with her wondrously beautiful name and face and all the rest. Think of Pomp watching the men watch her while the women watch the men, then everybody watching her long enough for everybody to wonder or know. Think of India coming through the room, parting the just-trying-to-get-by shitsuckers like me with her wondrous India face full of her look saying, Well, there you are, and there you are, you, Pomp.

Well, wherever you are, India, and whatever you are doing, it is Pomp, crawling back through the what is left me of the everyday you.

Her doing her everyday wondrous was nothing compared to her doing the other.

Pomp supposes you might be wondering a little about this other because old Pomp has wondered about it more than a little hisself. Using his eight years of land-grant schooling, and his just about fourteen years now of lawyering, his thirty-nine years on this great engine earth, what Pomp comes up with is every want gives rise to the opposite want, what Pomp calls this other.

Not much, is it?

Not much considering the higher schooling, these years.

Pomp did say middling. Pomp meant middling. Middling as Pomp is in looks and lawyering and all the rest, Pomp had India, at least for a while. Pomp wanders back to that while. Pomp often wanders back to that while when India was stretched out with nothing on on the bed. Pomp was eating an orange and listening to her breathing as she slept. There she was, and there she was, stretched out sleeping and adding up to wondrous. Yes, Pomp was eating the pulpy orange and listening to her and wanting her, wanting to be inside her and wanting her inside Pomp more than she was already. Pomp, the long ago fallen away Baptist, the not so good old good old boy, slipped some pulped-up orange up inside her, way up inside her, before stroking her all over, letting the orange squish around in our love juices before getting the orange back out and eating it.

Pretty good, huh? Pomp can even wander back so far as to tell you the special taste of that orange. Pomp can wander that far back, and Pomp can tell you how that pulped-up orange tasted like cuntsicle.

If you think that is something, think about this. Think about how Pomp's doing what he did gave rise to other wants, others he supposes should not happen, but do, and did.

. . .

Sometimes when Pomp is not able to sleep he heads down to the all-night Stop & Rob.

No doubt you already guessed why Pomp is not able to sleep, and yes, you are right, it is not the lawyering. The lawyering rolls along with little help from this lawyer. All Pomp does is tear out a few forms, hand them over to one of his girls, put on his best lawyering suit looking like it should belong to some lawyer somebody else, head down to the courthouse, talk his lawyer talk, stack up the checks.

It is not Pomp's health keeping Pomp from sleeping at night like a person should sleep. Considering the speed bump around his middle, some needed gum and crown work, his habit of trying to find some peace and sleep with the help of a George Dickel, or three, or more, his health is healthy enough. No, you are right, it is not the lawyering or his health that has him finding his not-so-good-old self all hours of the night at the all-night Stop & Rob.

At these hours, the wide and well-lit aisles are usually empty but for the working pimply high-school boy or the somebody shoplifting something or the other sort of somebody bored shitless come in to handle frozen chicken parts or the middling sort of nobody called Pomp who usually ends up with these chocolate-covered donuts reading these newspapers. Pomp knows you know what newspapers. These ones with the headlines and stories like: GIANT CATFISH ATTACKS SLEEPING BABY or MEN WHO DON'T BATHE ARE SEXIER SAYS SHRINK.

Check out the newspaper with the story about a three-hundred-year marriage where the couple were wed in nine past lives. Her and this life and wander-crawling around in the what was come to mind.

Well, maybe it is thinking such thoughts that will help Pomp close the gap on all the time we have been apart, put an end to this crawling back and thinking and feeling sick and feeling like a nobody who finds his shitsuckering self all hours of the night at the all-night Stop & Rob.

The same as Pomp said to you, there was this other.

We did other wants at Pomp's wanting. It was not the same as Pomp pressing his thirty-eight to India's wondrous head, although India certainly had her times of doubt. Like the time Pomp asked her to dress up in her black silk dress with the white polka dots, long black stockings held up with nothing other than a black garter belt, black shiny patent leather heels. She dressed up, and I drove us the next town over for what you can now stay home to see on your VCR, although back not so long ago you had to go over to the next town over late Friday nights.

The mayor, police chief and some others we knew were let in the side door while we were told to go in the front way. India balked at first, seeing those she knew and who knew her and knew her daddy and knew her daddy's daddy, but I wanted to, said I wanted to front way in or not, and in we went.

We sat in the dark with all those men knowing her and hers without any one of them saying anything to her other than what they said by not looking at us, by not looking at India's wondrous any time, but especially then.

After watching what was going on up on the big screen for a while, Pomp slipped his hand up India's long-stockinged legs, found her and brunswicked her the same as some hairy bowling ball until the mayor and those other men, most with eyes staring and mouths open the same as something murdered, were watching us instead.

The best part, the worst part, is India loving it all.

Feeling sorry for hisself and wandering some more back around in such thoughts and doing what Pomp told you Pomp does gets Pomp to work early. Pomp is in before his girls and while all is quiet except Pomp's heart and lungs, which are pumping away the same as if Pomp is running up the courthouse steps late in filing some high-paying company's claim.

Hearing his huff-pumping self like this and the whirring sound of the number going through the glass and copper telephone lines has Pomp wondering what to say.

"Hello, India's mom," Pomp says, trying not to show right off how Pomp is a professional something, mainly the professional horse's patoot Pomp knows his self to be.

"Who's this?" asks India's mom in her voice like India's voice except more mom-like.

"Pomp," Pomp says, waiting for the hang-up sound,

the sound of hard plastic on hard plastic. The hang-up sound does not happen. Pomp tells India's mom how the lawyering is going, without adding, with the no help from Pomp.

India's mom tells Pomp how the wedding went, how India married a Jew doctor, how India is studying to be a doctor herself.

Pomp does not remember hearing much after married except Pomp saying how a big case requires Pomp's traveling near to where India now lives, wherever that is, and how he would sure like to give India a call.

India's mom asks if Pomp is married.

Like the good lawyer Pomp is not, Pomp sidesteps the question by ignoring it and asking a question of his own. Pomp asks India's mom if she ever reads any of those Stop & Rob newspapers, the ones with the stories like: LIGHTNING MELTS ZIPPER, LOCKS MAN INSIDE PANTS.

Long quiet follows.

Long quiet follows before India's mom gives Pomp India's married-and-you-better-believe-Jew-sounding last name and India's telephone number.

By not saying good-by, Pomp makes it to the shitter without getting too much on his lawyering shoes, wing tips lightly chunked with chocolate-covered donut.

You remember Pomp telling you of the Pomp forgets whose party it was with everybody putting what they think, Pomp especially, were our most charming selves forward, and India with all her wondrous beauty coming in and putting a stop to it? Well, maybe this is what Pomp hopes in traveling to where India now calls home. In case it is not, there is always the thirty-eight.

Maybe Pomp will get his old self invited to supper using some of his lawyering, soft-talking skills.

Maybe Pomp will show his thirty-eight, putting the fear of something, the fear of a horse's patoot, in her Jew doctor husband.

Maybe, maybe not.

Maybe not since the thirty-eight is just the thirty-eight and nothing compared to memory. Think of India excusing herself from supper and old Pomp here asking Doc if he ever puts fruit way the hell up the wife. If Doc does, can Doc tell Pomp the taste of the fruit after Doc fishes the fruit back?

If this does not do the trick, maybe Pomp will tell Doc how Pomp can and watch Doc's expression go out.

Yes, yes, it is you know who, at his lawyering desk where all is quiet but for the chirping of these little birds ruining an all-night numbing, and the turning-over sound of the pages of one of these Stop & Rob newspapers, this newspaper with the headline: MAN GIVES BIRTH TO HIMSELF.

What do you make of that?

What do you make of you know who, hearing his heart and lungs sprinting and feeling his insides start to go while doing the dialing and hearing the whirring sound?

It is him, hearing two rings, then it is her.

"Hello," India says in her sleepy India voice with

Pomp nearly losing some of his insides and what little purchase on anything he has.

"Hello," India says again with this Pomp supposing her sleepy lying beside her successful-as-all-hell-doctor husband in all her everyday wondrous, all the wondrous Pomp once had until wanting some other, until wanting her past too, and then Pomp having her past too, Pomp having it all by having her tell me, despite tears and pleas, everything she ever did with anybody. No little anything was too little. What she wore when, their smells, her wishes, their sounds, until even with all her wondrous, all of India was not enough.

India forgave me.

India forgave me in her knowing what has taken all my years of schooling, lawyering, crawling around to right now come to know, and this is love like ours, love like mine, is its own undoing.

"Who's this?" India says.

Me, Pomp, not saying anything before softly hanging up.

LEGENDS

My boy reels his line in through the dark from the trees on the bank. He reels in and up a bare hook.

"Dad," my boy says, laying down his rod. "Who is the best, you know, you ever saw?"

"You, boy."

"Be serious, Dad," my boy says.

We drift over the slow opening ring of a single rise.

"Someone I served with," I say.

We drift on with the spoken part left at that.

What was never spoken by any of us who knew and were afraid to blunt it, or spook it, was that the Wiz was the best you ever saw. You knew the Wiz was the shit starting with what was inked on his helmet, those block letters spelling out SHAMAN, and THE WIZ. You knew seeing the long tube rig the Wiz carried on his back, what you first thought might be some sort of shoulder rocket, or maybe a long map case, and turned out to be the tube for what he called his ugly stick. See the Wiz—with the ground all blackened over and still smoking-up white—join up that nine-foot ugly stick of a smoke pole and head for the nearest bomb crater filled with a week's worth of monsoon rain, or a burned-off rice paddy, or some still burning river to false cast like a trick-rope artist at a rodeo. See him do that three or four times, then see him crank out fish, flop out some big bigmouth bass, and believe me, you knew.

We were almost all boys, not much older than my boy, but with nothing like boy lasting very long, at least not in those of us stepping in it every day. While the Wiz stepped in it the same as the rest of us, you could somehow never think of seeing him clothes-still-smoking dead. Seeing yourself dead is why most of us started drinking first thing, washing down the opium balls rolled around in your palm, doing what you had to do to dull the edge, to chill it so you would not have to feel sorry for anyone, mostly for yourself. The fear really came on when you turned around to see the sled you flew in on rear straight up, dip, then seemingly disappear as fast as light over the jungle.

We waited for after nightfall when Hand Job shagged us through the wire, kept us going out into the jungle until saying, "Get some."

We all clumped around the Wiz until Hand Job put his side piece in Okie Dokie's mouth and hiss-whispered, "Spread out!"

None of us who knew what we knew got far from the Wiz with his big night scope and his ugly stick and his all the rest of what he had. I went into some lie down and went to my place of no difference between awake and asleep. I went to my place for who knows how long before coming back to the Wiz working on his fly-tying knots close enough to reach over and touch him. The others were stretched out on their bellies with their hands and their faces night-painted up so the only white was the white of their eyes rolling like the eyes of scared ponies.

You listen to the soft patter drip of the jungle. You

listen to the ticking of Light Bulb's watch. You smell
the deep green rot the rain brings out. You smell your
own breath smelling like a dead snake sealed up in a
jar while trying to settle back into your place. You hold
yourself still in that place until something, until hearing
that suddenly-too-quiet-somewhere-deep-in-your-head,
until seeing something move in the clearing. Chill it.
Hold it. Chill it down while seeing something move
again. Lord, please make that something a monkey.
Make it some kind of night bird. Please make whatever
it is, Lord, anything other than what I know it is.
Somebody else sees it moving too and puts out a Fourth
of July sputtering-up that sends you back to being a boy
sitting on your sleeping bag spread out on the hood
of Daddy's car. Daddy and Mama and Sammy girl are
right next to you again, with all of us eating deviled-
ham-and-cheese sandwiches, slow chewing Mama's
sandwiches with upturned faces dead white in the fire-
work sizzle, flash, boom. Lay it back now. Hold it back.
It is all right. The Wiz man is right beside you, while
in the dead light of the floating-down flare, the snaketail
shower of sparks, the quiet of no lying to yourself now,
it is them. It is them and they are coming for you, slow
coming right at you, these three, four bareheaded and
barefoot boys with death held at the ready for you with
this being the one where you know you get it, Wiz or
no Wiz. See him screwing together his nine-foot rig, his
ugly stick. See how they are now so close there is no
time to get up, to run, to go so bad. You have to go so
bad the same as when you were a boy burrowed under
the pricker briars catching in your hair and on your

shirt. You have to go so bad burrowed down in these briars there is no way you can hold it, and, somehow, you hold it. You hold it and see Sammy girl run by without her seeing you. You hear Sammy girl's voice calling, "Olley, olley all come free." You stay burrowed down in these briars in your own let-go warmth and wet when somebody, the Canj Man maybe, lays out some heat and light. The others do and you do too, too fast squeezing off at the boys caught out in the open, caught in the rolling flash of man-made lightning, in the walking all around them of the Willie Peters, in the up above of the ghost-making flares in the great field of monsoon-clouded night. The boys are caught by our little high winds puffed into them and into the muck all around them. Our little winds jerk-blow them down into the muck where the boys stay. We pour more little wind into them, puffing up their hair and clothes and the muck around them. It stops with another flare parachute-sputtering down. The pock, pock of one of theirs starts up. Three or four of ours put out our answer back, sweeping back the dark until it stops, all of it, but for the crying out in the pillared-up white smoke of the Willie Peters, the over and over crying of what sounds like a little girl crying out.

I will thank you, Lord, by taking it, and taking it, and promising to make the most of every second of it, Lord . . . Where is the Wiz?

Another flare sparks over the clearing with two of ours crouch-running out, flopping down, getting up, running more into the hanging smoke. A burst of back and forth flash and the little girl crying stops.

"Okie Dokie, where's the Wiz?"

"Beats me, Wes, but look here," Okie Dokie says. "Looks like old Hand Job caught some."

The second lieutenant is a curled-up little boy. His helmet is overturned and the back of his head is a raised-up clot of chewed-up licorice.

"Thataway," Light Bulb says, looking at the boy lieutenant while pointing his sixteen behind us down a strip of muck.

You ease on down the slide of trail. You slip through the soft drip from up high. Easy does it over the little roots and the wait-a-minute vines. Hold your breath past the freeze-you-to-the-bone of what looks like a face and is a knot in a rocket-shattered tree. Ease down to the rushing-off of monsooned river.

Up to his knees in the sweeping through of the risen-up river is the Wiz doing the ancient waving of his wand. The Wiz lets the leader settle in first. The line snaps straight and the ugly stick spring bows with the Wiz coming up hard. Water streams up the leader, up the three feet of shearing, twisting, stopping, shaking the Wiz starts reeling in, cranking in, until the Wiz bends and one hand reaches under the rolling surge of river to raise high by the gills the biggest freshwater-finned-anything you ever saw. The Wiz—some sort of black statue in the deep jungle night—holds the fish up and out at arm's length. The Wiz dips that one-time fish back into the sweeping away river, and, with one quick twist, sets the fish free.

The yelp-barking of a fox somewhere in this moonlit night is what brings me back.

We have wind drifted out to the deepest part of the pond.

My boy is asleep among the everywhere risings. My boy, a gift better than I deserve, is asleep in the now so still I can hear the soft sucking sound of the big slow takes.

It was wasted lifetimes worth of being back before thinking of writing the Wiz and asking him how big he thought that fish was, and, then, never writing him or any of the others.

It was Light Bulb who wrote me. Light Bulb boy-scrawled how the Wiz was missing, could-be caught, could-be killed, and how there were rumors, and then how a brother in Recon told Light Bulb about seeing a naked black American boy way out in the boonies. That tall black American boy was fly whipping the night with the biggest damn ugly stick of a pole you ever saw. That black boy pulled out some kind of jump-up slippery water-god when the brother in Recon called out, yelled out, and that black boy was gone.

I reach for and pick up my boy's little pole, untwist the line, swing back as far as I can swing back and whir the weighted popper out and out into the night.

for Dort

ON RISING
AND SINGING:
A GUIDE TO
WHALE RIDING

The way in is first through the ear—the late summer night bug-buzzing on high. Underneath the buzzing is the clicking and whistling of the killers, their one to the other squeaking and lowing. The killers' language pulls the ears and the eyes down to the cement plot of blacker-than-night seawater. Under the topsoil of nightwater heaven showing the stars upside down are deep water moves. A shadow glides surface near before spiraling away, around, back again to bubble trails of breaking through, to plowing the three-acre grid of star field with six feet of notched-twice fin.

The two killers furrow on in their nightwater work: blowing saltwater smoke, rowing an eye upward, baring teeth as long and as white as sharpened piano keys.

You know their tune: hand signals, belly scratching, hunks of salmon helping you forget the *National Geographic* photographs of one of these killers blow-heaving himself onto an ice floe, his six tons tipping up the drifting ice table, sliding the white fur and the skittering black claw of polar bear down to the waiting snap and crunch of no more.

Knowing this, you make your way from the bug-buzzing of the grandstand down past the row upon row of no one here other than you and the killers, swoops of white saddle.

Up and out on the edge of the stage is the seawater-iron-smell of upturned earth after a spring rain; the up-closeness of these immense, snow-patched shadows.

Anything darker than star brings the killers up from trout-shadow size to what? To midget-submarine-size only longer, more tapered than the captured Japanese sub now landlocked-up out on the hometown green.

That size, but with none of the sub's slow-go hulk.

That size, but flash-squirming-quick-dwindle-diving back down to trout-fingerling size with you on the mark now, getting set now, letting go.

In this underwater world of no man breath, the dark and the cold are pulled on like another flapping tweed. Hair and the length of silk knotted about neck float loose, reminding you how living is a thing learned.

Follow your hair, break dark plane and float on your back.

The two killers are behind you with the star-diamonded water layering over the shiny black domes of their heads.

Slow bicycle-ride the legs.

Slap the night-cellophaned surface and the twice-notched killer, the bigger of the two, passes slab-solid and slick under palm.

Keep water-pedal pumping.

Keep slap-splashing until again, rising fast in boiling water, fish breath is blow-spraying forth in living song. The six-foot dorsal is now in hand and flying you up and through the saltwatery-silver foam cresting shoulders and chest in what feels like a dream of soaring and soaring until a headswing off and a rollover later and you are pedal-bobbing once again.

Swim over and along to the man-made edge with an olley-oop up to the weight and the drip of standing, to the listening and the looking for six-foot-notched sickle mowing black swells.

Here comes, up alongside here. Step on, hold on to the slip and smooth of Old Topnotch sliding away sea swell smooth and fast. You will not believe how fast, with the fear and the joy stretching you from the back of your shoulders to your belly to the all the way through and down you, with the night wind flapping your hair and silk and tweed, with the killers surrounding you with their bellows and clicks while dipping you away and keeling you over into splash.

In the darkness down on you, in the salt-soil layers of colder and colder, is silence.

The oldest way out makes you feel that you move at the heart of the world.

That is until a killer slides his six tons of deep-cave black and arctic-white swoop between your legs, slips notched hook into the groove of your spine before sea-bronc blasting droplets of silver into the star-flecked night where you are the rising and rising king of for-ever.

PASTORAL

Farmer Brown is a big man. We are speaking now of
the Farmer Brown who, from what I can tell, is no
longer a farmer, although he always says to call him
Farmer Brown. I do. I call him Farmer Brown, and I
say to you he is one big man.

Now as big a man as Farmer Brown is, and I do
mean big, he is not as big as he once was. For that
matter, none of us are as big as we once were. By us,
I mean the porcupines and me and Farmer Brown.
Other than the porcupines, none of us are as big as we
once were, and we are getting smaller.

Let us, us meaning you and me, let us back up a little
to when Farmer Brown first started getting smaller,
which was when Farmer Brown's big foot started getting bigger.

Farmer Brown's big foot, from his big toes to his big
knob of anklebone and up, started swelling up with the
skin going from white to yellowish to yellowish-green.
His big foot swelled up until the skin split.

About a day and a half later was when the sores
started eating at the wetness down inside where the skin
split.

Three days later, the sores were mostly black. By
then, there was also the stink. When the stink got to be
too much for Farmer Brown, Farmer Brown drove

himself in his Corvette over to the hospital where Farmer Brown's big toes were taken. Farmer Brown's big foot was taken. Farmer Brown's big leg up to the big knee was taken until some, not much, just enough to mention of Farmer Brown's big leg was left.

Farmer Brown says the doctors took what they had to take and sent the big rest of him back.

I know it is hard to believe, but Farmer Brown's Corvette is also getting smaller.

You may have seen Farmer Brown's Corvette out along one of these snowy back roads. If you have not seen the Corvette by now, the one parked over near the snowed-over and fallen-in chicken coop, you better hurry, for as we speak now, Farmer Brown's Corvette is getting smaller.

Farmer Brown is soon up, hopping around, sucking his crutches out of the mud and snow in the yard. Farmer Brown is lowering his big what is left of himself into what is left of his chewed-through Corvette.

Lowering himself is about as far as Farmer Brown gets with the Corvette until we fix Farmer Brown up with a sawed-off pool stick belted with two army web belts to the some, not much, just enough to mention stump of bandaged leg. By using the pool stick's bigger end, Farmer Brown can pretty much work the clutch and the brake.

Farmer Brown works the clutch and the brake the best Farmer Brown can.

Pastoral

. . .

Have you ever seen a grunting porcupine up close?
Have you ever seen a porcupine in a Corvette up close?
At this time of year with the snow drifting deep against
the fallen-in chicken coop, the porcupines come out at
night from wherever the porcupines come out from.
Click on the yard light and the porcupines are all over
the Corvette.

"Leave the porcupines alone," Farmer Brown yells
from his big bed.

Left alone, the porcupines keep coming back night
after night. With the day-to-day smaller of the way the
Corvette is now, smaller with most of the rubber on the
windshield wipers eaten away, and a lot of the leather
seats and armrests eaten away, the porcupines keep
coming back.

Have you ever seen a porcupine through a peephole
rear sight on a Gook piece?

You can pretty much guess how driving the getting
smaller and smaller Corvette with a sawed-off pool stick
for a leg is not easy.

Driving the Corvette paid for with the bundle Farmer
Brown says he saved up from his two loops—the same
Corvette that just this morning I discovered has some
of the wiring under the dash eaten away, the knobs on
the radio chewed off, the belt part of the seat belts
gnawed through—is now less easy for Farmer Brown to
drive, and not just because of the porcupines.

I guess it has been about three weeks since Farmer

Brown's big hairy hand, big hairy wrist, big hairy arm right up to Farmer Brown's big elbow were taken at the hospital.

It was this morning that Farmer Brown asked me to hacksaw the seven iron at the kitchen table.

If you think driving a disappearing Corvette with a pool stick for a leg is hard, you should see somebody try it with a pool stick for a leg and a golf club for a hand.

Jacob Bronstein is what is written in black pen on the photograph taken from the top drawer of the dresser near Farmer Brown's big bed.

What is anybody, other than Farmer Brown, doing going through the drawers of somebody else's dresser? Looking for ammo. Finding ammo. Finding a clip of long points for the big light Gook piece on the big bed that might be the same Gook piece in the photograph.

Jacob Bronstein is what is written on the back of the photograph of the young and gangly big Farmer Brown with the gangly neck and the gangly wrists. The gangly young Farmer Brown in the photograph is squatting on a tank or a half-track or whatever it is. The big light Gook piece Farmer Brown is holding up, the one that might be the same piece on the bed, looks tiny next to Farmer Brown. Farmer Brown is holding up the Gook piece and squinting up his big handsome face into a Gook sun. Farmer Brown is squinting up his big handsome face at whoever it is taking the photograph.

You can tell him whatever you want to call him, Jacob Bronstein or Farmer Brown, I call him Farmer

Brown with the big handsome face that was big and handsome right up to when the sores set in.

Farmer Brown sleeps in the light from the moon looking as if the moon crawled into the snow-covered branches of one of the big dead elms. The wind blowing in the dead elms waves the shadows of the creaking branches on Farmer Brown's big bed. The shadows wave on Farmer Brown. The shadows wave on those raised-up sores on what is left of Farmer Brown after more of Farmer Brown has been taken.

The shadows waving on Farmer Brown are about as big as his big other leg that has been taken all the way up to Farmer Brown's big hipbone. Watching the shadow branches wave over Farmer Brown makes it easy to almost believe the shadows are the big arm, the big leg, the other big leg that Farmer Brown no longer has.

Farmer Brown whimpers in his sleep while the shadows wave over my holding him, shushing him back to quiet.

"I hate to ask you only would you drive me" is all Farmer Brown says.

Outside is one of those winter mornings bright with the sun on new-fallen snow. Looking down I see the tracks from the night before. The tracks are all over the yard with the toed-in mark that could almost be the track of a barefoot boy.

The tracks all over the yard go up and on and inside

the snow-covered Corvette through the big hole eaten through the ragtop. The tracks go in to where the three-spoke steering wheel is eaten away.

Back upstairs, Farmer Brown has already worked out what we will do.

Farmer Brown is on the big bed. Farmer Brown's good one big arm is almost all the way in the big sleeve of his big army jacket. Farmer Brown's stink is worse than the stink has ever been. Farmer Brown stares at the water stains on the ceiling. Farmer Brown has worked out, even if I could have, me not having to drive Farmer Brown anywhere.

Sometimes, like times like tonight, when the blowing snow is a grainy sound against the farmhouse, in the big dead elms, against the snowed-under chicken coop, you can also hear the sound of grunting.

The grunting stops when you start crunching over and through the snow. The grunting stops when you get close enough to count the two, the four, the five porcupines. The porcupines look as big tonight as the porcupines have ever looked with their big porcupine eyes and their big porcupine yellow teeth and their big porcupine stink all over the next to nothing that is left of the Corvette.

Move in closer until the big stink rising off the porcupines is too much. Move in until the big porcupine stink is enough to keep you from moving in any closer, then move in closer. Move in until you are afraid to move in more without having something, a piece, in your hand. Hold the piece out until the barrel almost touches quill. Hold it and listen to the blowing grainy sound. Listen to the sound of the wind in the big dead elms. Listen to the big sound no matter how small you are of yourself still living.

I DON'T CARE
IF I EVER
GET BACK

We are in the rest of the world. The heat baby blankets me. The heat, the light are in the white stones of the parking lot. The stones chalk my hands.

"Put those down and give me your hand," my father says to me. The stones click back to stones. My hands are patted on my seat. The some small of me that is not my father is given to my father.

My father walks us over the hot of the dusted stones, around the silvered-glint off the cars. I am no bigger than where my father bends his legs. My shadow is a small shadow of his. His big shadow walks us, hand in hand, to these other boys as small as me, and bigger boys, and men in hats waiting in this light. The men smell of sweat, of hair under hats, of my Uncle Johnny Del's cigars. These men hold tickets the same as the blue ticket my father holds out. The man bigger on the wooden box than even my father's bigness takes our ticket. My father walks our big shadow over the bigger shadow of that man onto the cinder track. This width and grit of track widens over to the patter of water fountained, curves narrow around the green of the out-field curving around the closer red-clayed infield, comes wide back to this, our cinder-black self.

"What?" my father says to me. "What are you pointing at? Water? You want some water?"

My father has us in this world of mud. Water plops on puddled water, on mud, on dust. Bigger boys than

143

me call at other bigger boys, splash and spray. A man, big in his white-whites, in his black shoes cleating the cinders says, "Watch it, boys!" The bigger boys than me scatter back. The man spreads his big cleated shoes, bends. His cap is sideways on his big sweated head. His big throat apple is swallowed, and swallowed, and swallowed. The man bends up, sleeves his big man mouth, says to my father, "Go ahead, I'll hold it while you hold him."

My father flies me. My Red Ball Jets fly over rivers, lakes, pebbled boulders. Watered silver rains the dust of deserts. I close my eyes, reach with my mouth. The wet is slurped, breathed. Slurp this geyser again. This wet is too fast and much, bubbled big and much up my nose.

"Too much," my father says for me, saving me back down to the heat and light of standing.

In this light, we are so clearly seen for what we are.

The world is bleachered. My Red Ball Jets kick the darkness under the bleachers. Potato chip bags and paper cups spook white in the darkness under us. Spooking bigger boys than me call at one another, at me. My smallness of hand is inside the knuckle knots of my father's bigness of hand. My father is the rope keeping me from falling into the open darkness under us.

I watch up at my father's bigness watching out at the sunlit grass, the base paths where the men run in their white-whites. I watch up past my father's big face to the shadows under the roof. Birds coo white up in those shadows, birds, or the Father, the Son, the Holy Ghosts of spooking dead boys flapping on to Heaven. The Holy Ghosts of the boys wing through the pole of light hung across the shadows. The light is a giant's flashlight. The giant is looking for the Holy Ghost souls of boys the same as me, me, when my father lets go my hand to cup his big father mouth to shout, "Take him out, coach!" The Holy Ghost in me flaps out of me. The ghost of me rises near the birds watching me fly away from the beamed light of the giant. The calling boy souls in the darkness under my father's feet call at me more. I fly out from under the wide-slanted roof.

I float up in this blowing world of blue sky and light. I see down on my father in the bleachered rows, on the still living other boys, the bigger boys and the men in hats all toy-soldiered down. The men in their white-whites are smaller too. Those men run in and out of the big box shadows, over the greened-flat of the grass. I see the little rain of the small small boys spraying. I can see the ribbon of cindered track. I can see the whiteness of the parking lot, the sunlight off our car waiting for my father and for me.

Beyond our car, roads game board. Trees rug up green. Up from the green of the trees is the giant pencil point writing this is where God lives on Sundays. Tree tops nub under me. The whole world dollhouses down small.

Where we live is small fence, tarred roof, small-windowed. Rusty dog is smalled out in our yard. Rusty far away bark-barks up at me and is the only one not a giant, or God, who can see me now.

Mama—small as can be and still the Mama I came out of—comes out the back door of our house with a basket of what we wear. I can see my mama carry the basket past my barking brother. Mama's yellowed mama hair blows, as does what Mama clothespins up. Mama will save me. Mama of mine will wrap me saved in the socks, shirts, sheets Mama clothespins out. My Rusty dog brother will bite the giant, bark-bark at the calling boy souls lost in the darkness under the bleachers. What about my father? Mama will save the flying Holy Ghost me and say to me, "Who will save your father?"

Mama and Rusty and where we live littles all the way away. The world is sidewalk blurred under me as when my father carries me upside down. The world is blowing blue, clouds, light up above those tiny bugged-down men catching the tiny ball, those tiny men in their tiny men hats, these tiny boys smalier than me, small as me, the man my father and the afraid for him that is me beside him.

"I'm here" is what I say up to my father.

My father's bigness of arm hugs me into the darkness that is the father smell that is Mama's wash and him. My father hugs me safe in the sound of the world that is my father's heart.

A   N O T E   O N   T H E   T Y P E

This book was set in a digitized version of a type face called
Baskerville. The face itself is a facsimile reproduction of types cast
from molds made for John Baskerville (1706-1775) from his designs.
Baskerville's original face was one of the forerunners of the type
style known to printers as "modern face"—a "modern" of the
period A.D. 1800.

Composed by Creative Graphics, Inc.,
Allentown, Pennsylvania. Printed
and bound by R.R. Donnelley and Sons,
Harrisonburg, Virginia

D E S I G N E D   B Y   V I R G I N I A   T A N